Wallflower Games

Wallflower Games

LADY BE VENGEFUL

REVENGE OF THE WALLFLOWERS

DAWN BROWER

MG PRESS

"...when pain is over, the remembrance of it often becomes a pleasure."

— JANE AUSTEN, PERSUASION

Contents

EXCERPT: A WALLFLOWER'S STOLEN CHRISTMAS

EXCERPT: HER DUKE TO SAVOR

This is a work of fiction. Names, characters, places, and incidents are products of the author's imagination or are used fictitiously and are not to be construed as real. Any resemblance to actual locales, organizations, or persons, living or dead, is entirely coincidental.

Wallflower Games © 2024 Dawn Brower

Cover art by Mandy Koehler Designs

For everyone that doubts they can find love. May you find the one person meant for you

The Revenge Pact

A conclave of wallflowers. Was that the accurate term for what she had found herself a part of? There were several known wallflowers suddenly thrust together in one room together. A few ladies had exited the retiring room upon her entrance—not meeting her gaze as they departed. Lady Lilah Stevens was suddenly a pariah, and she couldn't fathom why. What the blazes had happened. Why were those ladies all whispering about her? She glanced around the room and her gaze landed on her sister's. Cora's eyes were filled with something? Sadness? Perhaps... Either way, it wasn't anything that made her feel good. The other three women shared a similar expression. She almost hated to ask...

"What is it?" she asked as anxiety filled her.

"The ton is filled with righteous blowhards," one of the women said. She had golden blonde hair and pale blue eyes the color of icicles shimmering against a skyline. She was pretty. Why was she a wallflower? "They like to think they're better than us, but are they really?" What was her name… Oh, that's right, she was that reprobate viscount's younger sister. Her name was Miss Emma Collins.

Lilah frowned. "We have all graced the walls at society functions together." She hated it as much as they did. "Why have we never spoken before?"

"Because wallflowers are both not seen nor heard," another said—Lady Victoria Spencer. She had rich brown hair and hazel eyes flecked with gold specs. Her lush figure was on the plump side, but she had a lovely, heart-shaped face.

"That doesn't mean we shouldn't speak to each other," Lady Selena Brooks said. She had brown hair streaked with gold, and her blue eyes were almost purple. She was the prettiest of them all, and from what she understood about her family, quite poor. Her dresses had seen better days, and the one she wore currently had to be one of her best. It was not fashionable at all. "Even wallflowers deserve friendship."

"None of this explains why you all had such grave expressions when I walked in," Lilah remarked. Or why those ladies had bolted from the room when she'd appeared.

"It's all my disreputable brother's fault," Emma said, then sighed. "I love him, but he's a bloody fool."

"He made some unfortunate statements about…" Cora bit her bottom lip.

"About what?" Lilah was confused.

"He made it sound as if…" Lady Victoria began, but her cheeks pinkened as if saying the words were the most scandalous thing she had ever done or would do.

"Oh just say it already," Lady Selena told them. "She needs to know."

Cora stared at the ground and mumbled, "He implied that you made advances on his person."

"Advances?" She barely knew the man. "What sort of advances?"

"Those of a more…" Emma cleared her throat. "lascivious sort."

"You know," Lady Selena said, waving her hand. "The naked sort. In the attempt to trap a gentleman into marriage."

Horror filled her. "I'd never…" She wouldn't

want a marriage that way. It would only end in disaster. "Why would he do such a thing?"

"I'm not sure he was even aware of what he was saying," Emma said, more to herself than anything. "He was quite foxed. I wonder if he mistook you for someone else?"

"I don't care what his reason was," Lilah exclaimed. "This will ruin me." Not that she had many prospects, but this would leave her with none.

"Makes one want to start plotting for real," Selena mumbled. "Wouldn't it be grand to be the ones leading the way for once?"

They all stared at her. "What do you mean?"

"Revenge," she said. "Sometimes it can be subtle, and sometimes it can be so blatant no one can ignore you ever again. Aren't you all tired of being swept aside?" Selena made her think of all the ways she'd love to make the Viscount of Harcrest pay for ruining her without a thought. Would his sister warn him if she did? She turned her gaze toward the woman in question.

Emma nodded at her. "I'd even help." As if she understood what Lilah had been thinking. "He should realize that he can't be so careless. He's an arse."

"Are we really going to do this?" Victoria asked in a meek tone. "I don't know…"

"Surely there is someone you wish to enact your own personal revenge on?" Lady Selena encouraged her. "Come on, tell us."

"There is one person…" She glanced at Selena imploringly. "You know who."

"My dear cousin," she said. "He's not the man you remember." She sighed. "But I understand. I've lived with him for the past several years. If not for him, I wouldn't have anything. My father certainly didn't ensure I'd have a good life. He died in debt and Foxcroft inherited that along with his own father's. I'll help you if you want me too, though." She glanced at them all. "We should make a pact here and now. Whatever we each need, no matter the reasons, for our revenge, we will help each other. There are no excuses accepted."

They all stared at each other, then nodded.

They stood in a circle around each other, full of resolve. They would do this and they wouldn't regret it. At least Lilah hoped they wouldn't. Sometimes a woman had to take action, and it was her turn. She would ruin a certain man's reputation beyond all repair. Let's see how he liked it being whispered about.

It didn't matter what each of their reasons was for revenge. The pact was formed, and they would see it to the end. Some times a leap of faith was required, and Lilah didn't regret making this one.

It was a warm spring day. Not that Miss Emma Collins could go outside to enjoy it. She was stuck indoors in a classroom. She would much rather be anywhere else. But no. She had to attend a finishing school. Her mother had insisted upon it. Her debut would not even happen for a couple more years. Why should she bother with this school? What did she have to prove to anyone? She had pleaded with her brother Henry, the Viscount of Harcrest, to allow her to remain at home. It was ultimately his decision. He had told her to mind their mother. In this instance, she knew best. If mother said she needed refinement, then by God she must.

She hated Henry for that and vowed to get even

with him. How could he have dismissed her concerns without even listening to what she had to say? How rude. So now she was at a finishing school so far from home, it would take weeks before she saw it. To make matters worse—almost no one liked her. Not that she had been given the opportunity to make friends. Most of the students hadn't even given her a chance. From the moment she had arrived, they had snubbed her. There were two in particular that were the worst. Miss Harriett Smythe and Lady Arabella Jones. Harriett and Arabella had decided she was beneath their notice, and the rest of the students had followed their example.

Which made Emma even more miserable.

"That will be all girls," Mrs. Ravenwood said. "I would like you to read Shakespeare's *The Comedy of Errors*." She stared at each one of them. "We will discuss it at length at our next meeting."

Emma wrinkled her nose. She did not want to read. Not on such a fine day. But if she didn't and came to class unprepared, Mrs. Ravenwood would flay her. Not literally, of course. But with a look and some well-placed words she would let her displeasure be known. Perhaps she could take the book outside. She could find a lovely spot to just relax and read. *The Comedy of Errors* was a play she had not previously read. It might even be enjoyable.

She gathered her belongings and went to her room. Her roommate was already there and sitting on her bed. Lady Fenella Carrick was a sweet girl. She had fiery red hair and pale green eyes. Freckles dotted her face and she had a shy smile. She was perhaps the only girl in the entire school that Emma liked. But then again, they had much in common. How could she not like her? The two pretentious girls that hated Emma seemed to dislike Fenella just as much.

"How was your literature class?" Fenella asked.

Emma sighed. "The same as always."

"That bad?" Fenella scrunched up her nose. "Were they terrible then?"

They didn't have all classes together. Fenella had deportment class while Emma went to literature. Emma wished that she had deportment with Fenella. Emma was unlucky in that she had many classes with Harriett and Arabella. Deportment was the worst class to have with those two.

"I am going to go outside to read," Emma said. "And forget about them. At least as much as I am able to."

"I wish you luck," Fenella said. "Those two will

not allow you to forget anything. They're harpies those two."

"I agree," Emma said, then sighed. "But I have to try. We are all confined to this school. There is no escaping them." She had written Henry again begging him to allow her to come home. He hadn't replied. Her reckless brother had probably holed up in his club and was drinking away his life, or maybe he had a mistress now. He was a scoundrel and seemed to have many women wanting to share his bed. Not that he mentioned them. Her brother wasn't that crude. No, the gossipmongers spread those tales. One day, he might stop being so reckless, but Emma had her doubts. "Are you going to stay here?" she asked Fenella.

"If you don't mind," she began. "I'd like to join you."

"Of course," Emma said. "I'd appreciate the company." She scrunched up her nose. "At least with you."

They strolled outside and through the gardens. They had a favorite spot. There was a large tree near the pond that gave them just enough shade not to bake in the warm sun, but enough light that they could read if they chose to. As they approached the pond, the echo of giggles greeted them. Fenella froze, and Emma stopped next to her. "It's them, isn't it?" Emma asked.

"I believe so," Fenella replied.

"Should we turn back?" she asked.

They wouldn't have any peace if they went to their usual place. Harriett and Arabella would make them miserable. It seemed as if that was their main purpose in life. To be irritants to those around them… Emma blew out a breath. This was not good. Not good at all.

"They probably won't be here long," Fenella suggested. "We could wait them out."

"Do you think so?" She frowned. "I don't know." She hated being so indecisive, but those two girls were that awful.

"Let's go," Fenella ordered. "We cannot allow them to scare us away. Otherwise, they will do that every time we cross paths with them." She glared at the Harriett and Arabella with contempt. "If we see them at a ball, are you going to be able to avoid them?"

"No," she said. That would be unlikely to happen. "They would not allow it."

"Then we cannot allow them to push us out of our favorite place. They know we come here. It is the only reason they are here."

Emma nodded. They headed toward the pond and the tree they liked to sit under. They never made it to the tree. Harriett and Arabella stepped in front of them.

"Where do you think you are going?" Harriett asked.

"Please move," Fenella said. "Allow us to pass."

"I don't think so," Arabella told her. She jutted her chin up in defiance. "We were here first. You leave."

"You do not own the pond and its surroundings," Emma told her. "We are welcome to relax here, the same as you."

"I don't think so," Harriett said. "Go, or I promise you will regret interrupting us."

Emma glared at them. "No. We plan to relax under that tree, and you two will not prevent that."

Arabella glared at her. Then she got a gleam in her eye that worried Emma. "All right. Go sit by your tree."

Emma and Fenella stepped past them. They didn't get far before they were shoved from behind. They both went tumbling into the pond. Emma flailed and spat out water. Fenella sank, and fast. Emma stared at her friend and dropped everything. She dove under the water to help her. She kept sinking. Her skirts flared out and she struggled to get to the surface. Finally, Emma got a hold of her and she yanked at her skirt, then pulled it free. She thanked God that her skirt was a separate piece and not secured to her shirt. She pulled Fenella to the side of the pond.

"She's not breathing," Emma said.

Harriett and Arabella stared. Neither one of them was moving. "Go get help, you bloody fools," Emma ordered.

Still, they didn't move. She didn't stop to make them get help. Instead, she focused on Fenella. She'd seen a servant breathe into another once, after they had nearly drowned. Emma didn't know if it would help, but she had to try. She pinched Fenella's nose and breathed into her mouth. After a few more attempts, she sputtered and spit out some water. Fenella's breathing was ragged, but at least she was alive.

"What happened here?" Miss Ravenwood asked.

"She fell into the pond," Harriett said. She had this innocent expression on her face, as if they hadn't pushed them in.

"You two," Miss Ravenwood said. "Go back to

the school and tell the headmistress we need assistance."

She turned to Emma. "You saved her life," Miss Ravenwood said. "Thank you."

"She's my friend," Emma said softly. "I had to try."

Miss Ravenwood nodded. "Go back to the school and change your gown. I'll see to her from here."

Emma did as she was told. But she didn't want to leave Fenella. Especially as it was the last time, she saw her. After nearly drowning, she'd been sent home. Emma had no friends left there. But she had many enemies. The top two: Miss Harriett Smythe and Lady Arabella Jones, and she vowed one day those two would pay for almost killing Fenella.

One

Emma stared down at all the invitations she'd finished addressing with a sense of satisfaction. It had taken a little convincing, but her brother had finally agreed to allow her to have a house party for Christmastide. Henry didn't know why she wanted to have one; however, Lilah did. At least to a certain degree. She hadn't outlined her revenge plan to Lilah, but she was one of the original wallflowers in the pact. Lilah had been the first one of them to seek her revenge.

It should have bothered her that Lilah aimed to achieve vengeance against her own brother, but Emma knew the truth. So she had agreed to help Lilah. Henry, in his drunken stupor, had fallen prey to an ambitious lady's scheming. While he hadn't been without culpability, it had not been entirely his fault. Lilah and Henry had fallen in love. She'd forgiven him—even before she'd realized that Lady Daisy Allen had been the true one behind her ruination.

But that revenge scheme is in the past. This was her chance. She would ensure that a few choice individuals understood the error of their ways. The invitations were officially coming from Lord and Lady Harcrest. So her quarry would not know that she was the one that had sent them. That was the beauty of her plan. No one would suspect a thing. She grinned with glee at the thought. This Christmastide she would get the greatest gift of all—her vengeance.

"Are they all completed?" Lilah asked. She stood in the doorway to the drawing room.

Emma nodded. "I sealed the last one a moment ago." She held up the stack of invitations. "They just need to be posted."

Lilah strolled over to the writing desk and held out her hand. "I will give them to Henry." She picked up the invitations. She tapped the stack. "Are you certain you wish to do this?"

"I am," Emma said. "There are some things I've never told you. Things I've told no one." Her years at finishing school still haunted her. How could she even begin to explain it to Lilah. Sometimes she did not understand it herself. "I need this."

Lilah nodded. She brushed back a loose strand of hair behind her ear. "I understand. You know I do." She sighed. "But sometimes revenge doesn't turn out how we wish it to."

Emma grinned. "And sometimes it gives you more happiness than you could ever have imagined." She wiggled her eyebrows. "Like finding the love of your life and finally living the life you always dreamed about."

"There is that," Lilah agreed. "But I am certain that isn't the norm."

"It's worked out all right for Cora and Victoria as well," Emma said. "I think revenge just might be the answer to finding one's true love," she said, wiggling her eyebrows."

Lila laughed. "That's ridiculous." She sighed. "Besides, Victoria didn't actually try for anything resembling revenge."

"That is true," Emma conceded. "Victoria just set out to seduce a man and fell in love."

"And Cora realized that revenge was the last thing she needed," Lilah said. "Now she's gloriously happy and loves Lord Thornton. Maybe even as much as I love Henry."

"You all are so happy it's a little disgusting to be around you at times." She grimaced. "This revenge business wasn't supposed to lead to a bunch of happy sods."

Lilah laughed. "You know you like seeing us all settled. Before you know it, you'll find love too."

"Now that is unlikely." Emma stood and went over to a window. She glanced outside and stared at the stark landscape. The colder months were not her fondest. She didn't even like snow much. Some did, but not her. It was messy and wet and made things just…inconvenient. She'd much rather a warm summer day and the colors of life to greet her—roses in full bloom, trees flush with green leaves, and a pond full of lily pads. The frozen land of winter she could do without. "I don't think I am meant to love anyone." She wasn't worthy of it. Her heart was empty. Nothing could fill it. She cared about her brother and even had a fondness for the other wallflowers. But loving a man enough to say vows? No. That was not happening. Ever.

"You never know," Lilah told her. "Sometimes you have to let fate help you along the way. I would never have given your brother a chance otherwise."

"I don't believe fate had any say in why you fell for Henry," Emma said, then chuckled. "He can be persistent. He wore you down until you have him no resistance. Then love just snapped into place like it was always there."

"Perhaps," Lilah said. "There is some truth there. He did seem to follow me around until I couldn't see any other man but him."

The grin on Lilah's face was so full of that unyielding love it made Emma ache. She didn't want love. That seemed too messy, but it still made her feel more than she wanted to. She didn't want to yearn. Emma wanted her revenge and then she could move on with her life. Love would only get in her way, and she would not allow such a fickle emotion to destroy what she had planned.

"That sounds like Henry." Emma forced a smile onto her face that she didn't feel. "He's nothing if not persistent. I am happy for you." And she was. Henry might have been a rogue, but he'd reformed when he fell for Lilah. He had gained Emma's respect with that devotion to Lilah. She turned away from the window and met Lilah's gaze. "But I need you to understand. I need this party. My revenge must happen. It's the only way I'll ever truly have peace." There were two ladies specifically that she would ensure felt as much humiliation and pain as she had. They had made her life hell, and it was her turn to give that back twofold.

"Your party will go forward," Lilah said. "I will take these invitations to Henry now." Resignation filled her voice as she spoke. Lilah may not agree with her, but Emma had her full support. They had made a pact after all. It had started with Lilah, and it would only end after they all had their own version of revenge.

"Good," Emma said. "I cannot wait for our guests to arrive." The anticipation that filled her was palpable.

Lilah left the drawing room. Emma went back to the window to contemplate what she had planned. Soon, her prey would be in her home. Then the fun would begin.

BLAKE SPENCER, THE MARQUESS OF ARDMORE, stared at the invitation on his desk. He'd received it two days ago, and he still didn't know if he wanted to attend. His friend, the Viscount of Harcrest, would be the host. This was a monumental occasion. Harcrest never had parties or balls, and now he was going to allow guests in his home during Christmas. He should go for that reason alone. To check on his friend and determine if he'd actually lost his mind. Had love and marriage changed the viscount that much?

A knock echoed through the room. "Pardon me, my lord," his butler, Draven, said. "But you have a guest. Should I see him in here?"

Blake glanced up and said, "Who is it?"

"I am certain I am welcome," another man said as he brushed past the butler.

"Certainly," Blake said, then grinned. "It's all right, Draven. His Grace is always welcome here." The Duke of Castlebury stood next to the butler with a wide grin on his face. His black hair was a little disheveled. There was a rough wind outdoors. Which was why he hadn't bothered to leave home. Blake couldn't abide the cold.

"Would you like refreshments, my lord?" Draven asked.

"Not at this time," Blake told him. "If that changes, I will let a servant know."

"Very well," my lord. Draven bowed and then left his study.

Castlebury strolled in and took a seat by his

desk. "I understand why you didn't order refreshments," he said in a droll tone. "But please tell me that doesn't extend to brandy. I could use a snifter or two. It's bloody cold outside."

Blake's lips twitched as he fought a smile. "I must ask why you braved the cold to come here. It must be important."

"I suppose it is," Castlebury said. "In a manner of speaking." He leaned forward and glanced at the invitation on Blake's desk. "I see you got one too." He gestured toward it. "Do you think he's lost his bloody mind?"

Blake shrugged. "Possibly." He went over to the bar and poured two snifters of brandy, then handed one to the duke. "But it's more likely he is willing to do anything to make his new wife happy. He's so in love it's nauseating to witness."

"Thornton is too," the duke said, then shuddered. "Apparently, he's been in love with that chit for years. I never knew."

"No one did." He drew in a breath. "Three of our friends are happily married. You don't think it's something that we could, you know, catch. Like a disease. I never would have thought Harcrest of all gentlemen would be susceptible to love and wed, but he was the first to fall."

"It was a surprise when he asked to use the chapel at Ardmore Abbey for an impromptu wedding." Blake took a sip of his brandy. "But as he is a friend, I agreed. I guess there is something about those Stephen's sisters. Two of our friend fell madly for them."

"Cora is my cousin by marriage now," Castlebury said. "Now that its come to light that Thornton's Mother is my aunt. Though we shouldn't publicly acknowledge that."

"But you will and have," Blake said. "Now the gossipmongers have truth to spread instead of speculation that Thornton is your bastard half brother. You two do look remarkably similar."

"As we are indeed family, that isn't such a surprise now, is it?" The duke sipped his brandy. "But that's not why I am here. Discussing my odd family isn't newsworthy."

"Why are you here," Blake said. "I must admit, I am surprised to see you in my townhouse. I didn't even realize you were in London."

"I've been here for a fortnight. I prefer my country estate. Fewer women vying to be my duchess there." He set his glass down. "I had intended to return there in a few days, but now I feel obliged to attend a house party."

"You're going?" Blake raised a brow. "I did not think you would accept the invitation."

"I feel obliged to," he said in a solemn tone. "As Thornton will be there and I'd like to spend Christmas with him. Cora will want to be with her sister, and it is at Lady Harcrest's house where this party is to take place. Everything is all tangled up and I don't like it."

"I don't either, my friend," Blake said honestly. "But what are we to do?"

"We are going to attend this party." Castlebury met his gaze. "And we are going to have each other's back. Neither one of us is going to find ourselves attached to a lady at the end of it. I will not be finding a wife at this house party."

Blake stared at him, shocked at the suggestion. "You don't actually believe that is a possibility, do you?"

"We have been at two house parties this year," Castlebury said. "And at them three of our friends fell in love. It could happen." He sighed. "And I do not wish it to. So we will go and we will stay by each other's side. At the end, we will return home as unattached as we are now.

"All right," Blake agreed. "We will do that. I don't wish to have a wife either."

"Good," Castlebury said. He drained his brandy, then stood. "I'll make the arrangements and we can travel together. Maybe we can find a reason to depart early too. I don't want to remain at Harcrest Manor longer than we need to be. We can find some sort of convenient excuse to take our leave."

"I will have my valet prepare my trunks. When will we leave?"

"Tomorrow morning," the duke said. "If that is all right with you." He stood and set his empty snifter on a nearby table.

"It is," Blake said. "I'll be ready." Not that he wanted to go, but at least they had a plan.

The duke nodded and left the room. Blake looked at the invitation again. What was it about house parties, anyway? Why had his friends fallen in love at the last two? He must find discover why, so he didn't fall prey to that befuddling emotion. He would never be so weak as to need a woman or go mad without her. Not him. Not ever.

Two

Emma tingled with anticipation. Everything was falling nicely into place. Every one of the invitations she'd sent had been accepted. The manor would be full for Christmastide. It would be marvelous, and not just because her revenge would finally come to fruition. Her friends would be there and they could celebrate together. She'd only had one friend before the wallflowers had sealed their pact, and that friend she hadn't seen in years. That too, would change soon. At least she prayed it would.

She strolled into the sitting room and grinned. They were all there. The other guests wouldn't arrive for another day or two, but the most important invitations went to the four ladies waiting for her—Lilah hadn't received an invitation since, technically, she was the hostess. They were all drinking tea and chatting as if no time or distance had separated them. "Hello," she said, then went over to join them. "I'm so happy to see everyone."

Victoria grinned. "We are glad to be here." She patted the side of the settee next to her. "Come sit. Tell me everything. I want to know your plans."

Emma went over to the settee and sat next to Victoria. She should have poured herself a cup of tea first, but hadn't thought of it. Perhaps she'd have some later.

"We all want to know," Cora said, then sipped her tea. "I was excited when the invitation arrived. I suspected this was a scheme of yours. Especially, since Lilah hates socializing." She wrinkled her nose. "Though bravo for having her be the hostess. You know all those harpies are savoring at the opportunity to see if Viscount Harcrest is still besotted with her."

Lilah rolled her eyes. "That man adores me," she said with a contented sigh. "I am truly fortunate to have won his heart. Though if you had asked me that prior to that house party, I would have thought you all mad."

"Indeed," Emma agreed. "The truth is that my

brother is the fortunate one. He could have ended up married to the likes of Lady Daisy Allen."

"She's awful," Selena said. "He is indeed lucky that she didn't sink her claws into him." She took a sip of her tea. "Has anyone heard what's happened with her? Anything new?"

"As far as we know," Emma said with an evil grin. "She's still at that finishing school her father sent her to." Emma was all too familiar with that finishing school as she'd attended it. Lady Daisy was likely just as awful as the girls Emma had attended with. She would likely fit in famously. Though she wished with her whole heart that Lady Daisy was not treated well. Because otherwise that girl would never learn and would continue to believe herself above everyone. Just because she was the daughter of a duke did not mean she could be so awful to those around her.

"I still think she deserved worse than that," Lilah said. "She nearly ruined my life. All because she thought Henry belonged to her. She was willing to do anything to have him. It's just...wrong."

"It is," Selena agreed. "But she didn't win. That is what you need to remember." She nodded toward Emma. "And that's now why we are here. This house party is for her to get her revenge." She leaned back and stared at Emma. "What do you need from us?"

"Nothing," she said. "But I suppose I can tell you my plans. Just in case help is needed that I haven't already foreseen."

"Go on," Lilah encouraged. "What do we need to know?"

Emma stood and went over to the teacart to pour herself a cup of tea. She put two lumps of sugar into her cup, then stirred slowly. She wasn't certain where to start or what she should tell them. How much was too much? She sighed and went and sat next to Victoria again. Emma sipped her tea and then closed her eyes briefly. When she opened them, all four of her fellow wallflowers were staring at her expectantly. "There is much I've told no one," she said. "I mentioned as much to Lilah when we were discussing the invitation."

"You did," Lilah confirmed. "Are you ready to discuss it now?"

"Not entirely," Emma said. "It has to do with my own experience at finishing school." She hated thinking about that time. "Henry thought it would be good for me to go. I was terribly shy back then. I begged him to let me stay home. In some ways, it helped me to accept myself. I did grow bolder because of my time there." She'd had to. If she hadn't started to stand up for herself, she might not have survived that school. "But I am afraid I was always destined to be a wallflower." Emma didn't do well in social situations.

"What happened to you at school?" Victoria asked.

"It wasn't one thing," Emma said. "A lot happened at school, some of it I'd rather forget." She inhaled sharply. "But I cannot. It's always there." She glanced away from them. "Two girls made my life miserable there. They are the ones I want revenge on, and I intend to have it."

"Who are they?" Selena asked.

"Yes," Cora said. "We want to know."

Emma shook her head. "Not yet," she said. "When I need your help, I'll let you know. But I want to do this on my own for as long as possible. I need them to understand how their cruelty affected me."

"And you shall," Lilah told her. "Are you going to tell us what you have planned, even if we do not know who?"

She shook her head. "I cannot," she said. Partly because she didn't have it all quite worked out. But it had a lot to do with humiliation. She had to ensure all the targets arrived so she could start pulling their strings. "It's too complicated and I am afraid if I start speaking my plans it will all unravel."

Selena laughed. "All right. Keep your secrets. We will be here if you need us."

Emma breathed a sigh of relief. She sipped her tea. These women were the reason she had the courage to see this through now, when before she wouldn't have been able to. She smiled at them, just content to spend the afternoon in their company. Soon the manor would be overrun with guests and times like this would not be so easy to find. So, she relaxed and enjoyed their company. Revenge schemes could wait until the guests arrived.

BLAKE STROLLED INTO HARCREST'S STUDY. THE viscount was behind his desk, going over some ledgers. Harcrest frowned at the books on his table. He could commiserate with Harcrest's frustration. There was plenty of time he'd stared at his own accounting books with the same expression on his face. He didn't enjoy that part of running his estate, either.

"That bad, is it?" Blake said in an amused tone.

Harcrest glanced up and met his gaze. There was a glazed look there that he shook away. "It will be fine," he said. "I just have to sort out a few discrepancies." He closed the book and gave Blake his full attention. "You're here earlier than expected."

"You can thank Castlebury for our timely arrival," he said casually. "He stopped by my town-house and suggested we travel together since he was in town."

"He came?" Harcrest asked, surprised. "I must admit, I didn't think either of you would make the journey here. I wouldn't blame you if you had decided to remain home."

Blake shrugged. "My sister is here," he said. "And Castlebury mentioned that he would like to see his cousin. We're all family, in a sense. So why not come and spend Christmastide here? It was no trouble, and Castlebury is an excellent traveling companion."

The viscount nodded. "That makes sense." He leaned back in his chair and sighed. "I'm actually surprised that Emma wanted to have a house party. She wasn't a wallflower without reason."

"This was your sister's idea?" He frowned. "What reason did she give you?" Blake was as surprised as the viscount. He wasn't that familiar with his sister. They hadn't had a chance to become acquainted over the years. Though he suspected his own sister had become friendly with her. Perhaps he should make a point to have a conversation or two with Harcrest's little sister while he was there. To at least discover what Victoria might see in her.

"She said she missed her friends." Harcrest stood and walked over to the bar in his study. He poured a snifter of brandy. "Would you like one?" He asked.

"Yes," Blake said. "Please."

Harcrest handed him his snifter of brandy and took a sip from his own glass.

"Why didn't she just invite her friends, then?" Blake sipped his own brandy. "Why have so many guests at Christmas?"

"That's what I said." He sighed. "But Lilah took her side and I cannot argue with my wife and my sister." He drew in a breath. "Well, I could, but I don't like having disagreements with my wife. That never leads anywhere pleasant." He brought his glass to his lips for a drink. "And I would like to have a more, shall we say, pleasurable time with Lilah."

Blake laughed. "I can see why you would." He sipped on his brandy and wandered over to a window. Snow fell lightly outside, but not enough to raise any concern. It would barely blanket the ground once finished. "Did Lilah give a reason for her support of Emma's wishes?"

"No," Harcrest said. "But I didn't expect her to. Though it did surprise me. Lilah hates society as much as Emma. There has to be some reason there."

That was interesting… He turned to glance at Harcrest. "Do you have suspicions about what that reason might be?"

He shook his head. "I'm almost afraid to ask." He joined Blake at the window. "Those women…" He frowned. "I hate to refer them as such, but it is the truth. Or was… They were all wallflowers. They must have become acquainted while gracing the walls together at those societal functions. They could have discussed almost anything. They are all intelligent enough. That should scare all the gentlemen of the ton witless."

Blake considered that. Had they plotted something? If so…what? Perhaps this house party would be far more interesting than he had thought. At the first opportunity, he would have a conversation with Miss Emma Collins. He might not be able to discern the truth from one little discussion, but it would be a start. He would also take the opportunity to observe the other wallflowers. Had they hatched this scheme months ago? Long before that original house party? Was that how his friends ended up married to three of them? If so, he would definitely have to be on guard. He would not find himself married to a wallflower. How preposterous…

"You could be right in your supposition," Blake conceded. "Or you could be seeing something that isn't there." He shrugged. "I do not think we will ever truly know either way."

"Perhaps," he said. "I could ask my wife."

"Do you believe she'd admit to it?" Blake arched a brow.

"If I asked her?" Harcrest frowned and turned away from the window. Blake turned and watched as he went back and sat at his desk. He set his glass of brandy down. "Yes, she'd tell me the truth."

"Then why haven't you asked?" Blake had never been so confused.

"Because maybe I don't want to know. If I asked her and she told me something I didn't like, then what would I do then? Would I stop them from what they have planned? Does it even matter?" He sighed. "I'm not a fool. That whole mess with Lady Daisy Allen—I knew then that they had been scheming. It was quite obvious. If they hadn't, I might not have Lilah for a wife now. That other harpy might have gotten her way."

"Would you have married her?" Blake asked. He was a little surprised at the direction this conversation had turned toward.

"I would not have wanted to." Harcrest picked up his brandy once more. "Her father is a duke. He'd have ruined me. I have Emma to consider."

Blake nodded. "Perhaps it is best if you do not ask." But that did not mean that Blake had to remain in the dark. He wanted to know what they planned. "I'll leave you to your ledgers. We can talk more later." He set his brandy down, unfinished. He had some planning of his own to do, starting with how he would corner Emma and discover all of her secrets

Three

All the guests were there. Even her extra special guests that she had invited for a reason other than a Christmastide house party. The next fortnight would be filled with fun, games, and tricks…with a little revenge sprinkled in for good measure. Today she was planting seeds and gaining conspirators—albeit unknowingly. They would agree to do little favors for her without even realize what she'd asked of them. All the guests were there. Even her extra special guests that she had invited for a reason other than a Christmastide house party. The next fortnight would be filled with fun, games, and tricks…with a little revenge sprinkled in for good measure. Today she was planting seeds and gaining conspirators—albeit unknowingly. They would agree to do little favors for her without even realize what she'd asked of them. If all went well, she'd have them all doing their bidding.

She strolled into the parlor. They were supposed to be playing games. That was the entire reason for the gathering. She had other games in mind, and none of them had a thing to do with cards. Emma glanced around the room and looked for her first target, um, guest. When she located Viscount Clouston, she grinned. Perfect. He was alone. She made her way through the throng of guests until she pretended to trip and fall. The viscount reached out to steady her.

"Pardon me, my lord," she said. Emma glanced up at him beneath her lashes. The viscount had sandy brown hair and eyes that matched. The brown on brown should have been dull, but on him it added to his male beauty. He had been one of the gentlemen that had caught her attention when she'd first had her debut. Her gaze had landed on him, and she nearly licked her lips with appreciation. He had high cheekbones and full, very kissable lips. His simple brown eyes were far prettier than they should have been on a man, and framed by dark lashes that gave him a dreamy appearance. "I don't know what happened."

"I'm certain the fault was mine," he said in an earnest tone. Emma didn't believe he truly was though. "Are you all right?" She almost sighed. He really was a gorgeous man, but she also knew that he could be cruel. She'd felt that sting firsthand.

"I assure you, my lord," she said in a coy tone. "It was a mere moment of clumsiness. Something must have caught me off balance. It was a moment, nothing more."

"Then allow me to escort you around the room. It would make me feel more at ease if I am there to catch you if you should fall again." He tilted his lip upward into a decadent smile. That only made him even more beautiful. It would have sent a lesser woman's heart all aflutter, but Emma was made of sterner stuff. She had plans for this gentleman, and it had nothing to do with seduction. At least not her seduction.

"I couldn't possibly ask that of you." She smiled shyly. Emma was a wallflower. She was not supposed to have any wanton abilities. So she played into Lord Clouston's expectations.

"I am offering my services," he said. "As a

gentleman." If he were a woman, he'd be batting those perfect eyelashes of his coquettishly. "I insist."

"Very well," she agreed. "It wouldn't hurt to have a gentleman such as you by my side."

He fell into step next to her as she continued into the room. She didn't say a word. Not yet. She allowed him to become comfortable by his side. She had to keep her tone in the same timbre and feel of his, and mirror his actions to make him feel as if they had something in common. Once he looked toward her as someone that he could trust, because in his mind he knew her, then she'd start the rest.

They reached the other side of the room and stopped next to a group of gentlemen playing whist. He frowned as he met another gentleman's gaze. "I say, Marlinton," he began. "Should you be playing whist? You're a terrible player."

The Earl of Marlinton rolled his eyes. "I am not that horrid." He groaned. "Really, Clouston. You're supposed to be a friend and support me in my endeavors." Where the viscount was dark, Marlinton was a golden god. He had blond hair that always looked as if it were kissed by the sun, and eyes so blue that they reminded Emma of the Serpentine on a hot summer day. They were the best of friends, and where one was, the other could be located nearby.

"I am a friend," he said. "And as your friend, I am reminding you of your limitations."

Emma patted his arm. "You're a great friend, my lord." She turned toward the earl. "You should heed your friend's advice, my lord."

Marlinton narrowed his gaze. "And who the bloody hell are you?" And where Clouston acted the gentleman, the earl did not. He was a bloody sod. Pretty to look at, but nothing but rudeness spilled from his mouth.

"Surely you remember Miss Emma Collins," the viscount chastised his friend.

Emma held back a grin. This was going according to plan. She'd have their help. Both of them, when she needed it. She was playing a long game, though, and this was only the beginning. They were not ready for her to start asking for those favors.

The earl narrowed his gaze. "Miss Collins?" He tilted his head to the side. "Yes, I believe I do." He didn't remember her. The only reason that the viscount did was because her brother hosted this house party.

"It's a pleasure to make your acquaintance

again, my lord." She smiled at him. With him he'd appreciate a little wantonness, so she nibbled on her bottom lip, and peered at him through lowered lashes—a mix of sin and innocence. She knew her targets, and she wanted them to be her willing slaves. They were not the ones she intended to enact her revenge on. They were going to be the pawns in a game where she was their queen. They'd knock down her enemies to nothing by the end of the house party.

"The pleasure is all mine," the earl said. He set his cards down. "I'm out." He stood and said, "There has to be something more entertaining at this house party. Perhaps you can help us find it."

"I don't know…" She glanced around. "I promised Lady Harcrest I would act in her stead during the parlor games."

The earl leaned down. "But what fun is that?" He met her gaze, then winked. "Let's find something else more entertaining."

"Very well, my lord," she acquiesced. "I might be able to oblige you." She glanced at the viscount. "Will you be joining us then?"

"Of course." The viscount grinned. "I promised to stay by your side."

Wonderful. She had two gentlemen, and some games to set into motion…

Blake followed Emma around the room with his gaze. She didn't know what game she was playing, but he'd bet his entire unentailed inheritance those two gentlemen didn't know that she led them around as if they were still in leading strings. Fools. He sat in the corner sipping brandy, when all he wanted to do was retreat to the game room and pretend, he wasn't attending a house party. He should go find Castlebury and demand he play a game of billiards with him. Of course, the duke was absent from the afternoon's entertainment. Parlor games were far too tame for them. They would not have normally played them. At his own house party, Victoria had handled all the entertainment and he'd stayed absent as much as possible. Unless his sister had required him for something, he let her plan the entire bloody thing. He hadn't wanted the party after all.

Emma left the room with her two suitors. Wasn't she supposed to be a wallflower? How had she ensnared those two sops to do her bidding? He narrowed his gaze. They really did seem to be besotted with her. Something wasn't right there. He drained his brandy and set the empty glass down on a nearby table. He intended to follow behind them and see what she was up to. Blake still thought there was something odd going on with the wallflowers, former and still. Though looking at Emma now, he had to wonder why she'd ever been a wallflower to begin with.

He had never paid much attention to her before. That had nothing to do with her. Blake didn't pay attention to any innocent lady searching for a husband. Especially as he didn't intend to wed. But now that he saw her, he had to appreciate what a beauty he'd found. She had golden blonde hair and striking blue eyes. Her heart-shaped face looked delicate, but those pouty lips—those were pure sin. It was like an angel come down from the heavens with the purpose of seduction. If she were not Harcrest's sister, and an innocent, he'd find out for himself if she was as wicked as she seemed. Hell, he might anyway.

Blake kept a leisurely pace as he followed them. He could hear their discussion, and he almost laughed. She played them both with ease and neither of them realized it. She strolled into the game room. At least it was empty. "Here you go, my lords," she told them. "You can play billiards in here."

"We could," they both said in unison. "But what will you do?"

"I can sit over there and watch." She had that innocent tone in her voice. "I'm not much for games. But if you need me for something, I'll still be here."

They went over to the side and grabbed cue sticks and set the game up to play. Once they started, Blake strolled into the room. "Ah," he said. "I missed a chance to play."

"You can play the winner, my lord," Emma said. She narrowed her gaze on him. Was she determining the best way to handle him, too? She would be in for a surprise.

"I'll just have a drink and watch. Not sure I want to play." He went to the bar and poured a glass of brandy. On a whim, he poured a second glass and took it over to her.

She stared at it, then at him. "I don't…"

"Take the drink, Miss Collins," he said. "I think you have earned it."

Tentatively, she reached up and took the brandy. "And why have I earned it?" She lifted a brow.

He sat in the seat next to her. "I must say, I was surprised at how easily you have them wrapped around your finger." Blake took a drink of his brandy. "Those two are usually not led around so easily."

She turned away from him as she said, "I'm not certain I understand your meaning."

He held out his glass toward the two men playing billiards. "They're not young fools, but you're making them out to be just that." Blake stared at her. "What is your secret?"

Emma stared at her glass of brandy and brought it up to her lips. She sipped tentatively. Blake nearly smirked, but held it back. She grimaced. "This is awful."

"But it has a nice burn," he told her. "I thought you might appreciate it." He smiled as he took another drink. It hadn't escaped his notice that she ignored his question.

She took another drink, then another. Then she licked her lips. Blake nearly groaned. She had the best lips. He wanted to taste them and lick the brandy off those tantalizing lips. "It grows on you," she finally said.

"That it does," he agreed. His lips curled up into a wicked smile. "Many things do."

"Why are you here?" she asked him.

"At the manor or this room?" he asked. Blake thought he might already know which, but he wanted her to be bold.

"This room," she said, then rolled her eyes. "I know why you're at the manor. I wrote all the invitations. If I didn't know you were on the guest list, I'd be a bloody fool."

That was interesting too… He hadn't realized that Lady Harcrest hadn't addressed all the invitations. "I am here," he said. "In this room to uncover what scheme you are concocting." He emptied his glass. "Because I have no doubts, there is one."

"Even if there is," she began. "It has nothing to do with you."

"That may be true," he told her. "But I'll still investigate. I don't like secrets."

She sighed. "What will it take to make you go away?"

Blake thought about it. She wouldn't let him in on her secrets willingly. But perhaps she'd play a game with him. "How about a wager?"

"A wager?" She frowned. "What would we make a wager on?"

"I want to know what this is all about." He motioned toward the earl and viscount playing billiards. They hadn't even bothered to address him when he entered the game room. They were that focused on each other. "So, if I discover what it is you are plotting," he told her. "Then I will win."

"And if you don't—I win?" she finished.

"Exactly," he said, then grinned. "Finish your brandy, love. It is rude to waste good spirits."

She glared at him. "And if you win, what do you want from me?"

Blake only wanted one thing from her. He wanted her naked and tied to his bed, where he could pleasure her all night long. He wanted to taste every inch of her delectable skin and hear her moan with all the exquisite torture he'd deliver her. But that was asking too much. She'd never agree to it. "Why don't we make this simple," he said. "The winner will get a boon of their choosing from the winner."

"I won't allow you to seduce me," she warned.

"Sweetheart," he said. "I wouldn't need a wager to seduce you." He leaned in close so that only she'd be able to hear him. "You'd be in my bed before you realized that you ceded everything to me." He stood. "So, do we have a wager?" He lifted a brow. "Or would you rather I take my concerns to your brother?"

"All right," she said in a resigned tone. "You have your wager."

"Excellent," he said. "I will leave you to your young bucks for now." He wiggled his eyebrows. "Happy scheming, love."

Blake left her alone in the game room. He'd find out more later. He had enough for now, and he finally had begun to enjoy this house party. All because of one little vixen that he wanted to kiss desperately, and he fully intended to at least give in to that urge before the fortnight was over.

She strolled into the parlor. They were supposed to be playing games. That was the entire reason for the gathering. She had other games in mind, and none of them had a thing to do with cards. Emma glanced around the room and looked for her first target, um, guest. When she located Viscount Clouston, she grinned. Perfect. He was alone. She made her way through the throng of guests until she pretended to trip and fall. The viscount reached out to steady her.

"Pardon me, my lord," she said. Emma glanced up at him beneath her lashes. The viscount had sandy brown hair and eyes that matched. The brown on brown should have been dull, but on him it added to his male beauty. He was one of the gentlemen who caught her attention when she first had her debut. Her gaze had landed on him, and she nearly licked her lips with appreciation. He had high cheekbones and full, very kissable lips. His simple brown eyes were far prettier than they should have been on a man, and framed by dark lashes that gave him a dreamy appearance. "I don't know what happened."

"I'm certain the fault was mine," he said in an earnest tone. Emma didn't believe he truly was though. "Are you all right?" She almost sighed. He really was a gorgeous man. But she also knew that he could be cruel. She'd felt that sting firsthand.

"I assure you, my lord," she said in a coy tone. "It was a mere moment of clumsiness. Something must have caught me off balance. It was a moment, nothing more."

"Then allow me to escort you around the room. It would make me feel more at ease if I am there to catch you if you should fall again." He tilted his lip upward into a decadent smile. That only made him even more beautiful. It would have sent a lesser woman's heart all aflutter, but Emma was made of sterner stuff. She had plans for this gentleman, and it had nothing to do with seduction. At least not her seduction.

"I couldn't possibly ask that of you." She smiled shyly. Emma was a wallflower. She was not supposed to have any wanton abilities. So she played into Lord Clouston's expectations.

"I am offering my services," he said. "As a gentleman." If he were a woman, he'd be batting those perfect eyelashes of his coquettishly. "I insist."

"Very well," she agreed. "It wouldn't hurt to have a gentleman such as you by my side."

He fell into step next to her as she continued into the room. She didn't say a word. Not yet. She allowed him to become comfortable by his side. She had to keep her tone in the same timbre and feel of his, and mirror his actions to make him feel as if they had something in common. Once he looked toward her as someone that he could trust, because in his mind he knew her, then she'd start the rest.

They reached the other side of the room and stopped next to a group of gentlemen playing whist. He frowned as he met another gentleman's gaze. "I say, Marlinton," he began. "Should you be playing whist? You're a terrible player."

The Earl of Marlinton rolled his eyes. "I am not

that horrid." He groaned. "Really, Clouston. You're supposed to be a friend and support me in my endeavors." Where the viscount was dark, Marlinton was a golden god. He had blond hair that always looked as if it were kissed by the sun, and eyes so blue that they reminded Emma of the Serpentine on a hot summer day. They were the best of friends, and where one was, the other could be located nearby.

"I am a friend," he said. "And as your friend, I am reminding you of your limitations."

Emma patted his arm. ""You're a great friend, my lord," she said, turning toward the earl. "You should heed your friend's advice, my lord."

Marlinton narrowed his gaze. "And who the bloody hell are you?" And where Clouston acted the gentleman, the earl did not. He was a bloody sod. Pretty to look at, but nothing but rudeness spilled from his mouth.

"Surely you remember Miss Emma Collins," the viscount chastised his friend.

Emma held back a grin. This was going according to plan. She'd have their help. Both of them, when she needed it. She was playing a long game, though, and this was only the beginning.

They were not ready for her to start asking for those favors.

The earl narrowed his gaze. "Miss Collins?" He tilted his head to the side. "Yes, I believe I do." He didn't remember her. The only reason that the viscount did was because her brother hosted this house party.

"It's a pleasure to make your acquaintance again, my lord." She smiled at him. With him he'd appreciate a little wantonness, so she nibbled on her bottom lip and peered at him through lowered lashes —a mix of sin and innocence. She knew her targets, and she wanted them to be her willing slaves. They were not the ones she intended to enact her revenge on. They were going to be the pawns in a game where she was their queen. They'd knock down her enemies to nothing by the end of the house party.

"The pleasure is all mine," the earl said. He set his cards down. "I'm out." He stood and said, "There has to be something more entertaining at this house party. Perhaps you can help us find it."

"I don't know..." She glanced around. "I promised Lady Harcrest I would act in her stead during the parlor games."

The earl leaned down. "But what fun is that?"

He met her gaze, then winked. "Let's find something else more entertaining."

"Very well, my lord," she acquiesced. "I might be able to oblige you." She glanced at the viscount. "Will you be joining us then?"

"Of course." The viscount grinned. "I promised to stay by your side."

Wonderful. She had two gentlemen, and some games to set into motion…

BLAKE FOLLOWED EMMA AROUND THE ROOM WITH his gaze. She didn't know what game she was playing, but he'd bet his entire unentailed inheritance those two gentlemen didn't know that she led them around as if they were still in leading strings. Fools. He sat in the corner sipping brandy, when all he wanted to do was retreat to the game room and pretend, he wasn't attending a house party. He should go find Castlebury and demand he play a game of billiards with him. Of course, the duke was absent from the afternoon's entertainment. Parlor games were far too tame for them. They would not have normally played them. At his own house party,

Victoria had handled all the entertainment and he'd stayed absent as much as possible. Unless his sister had required him for something, he let her plan the entire bloody thing. He hadn't wanted the party after all.

Emma left the room with her two suitors. Wasn't she supposed to be a wallflower? How had she ensnared those two sops to do her bidding? He narrowed his gaze. They really did seem to be besotted with her. Something wasn't right there. Blake finished his brandy and placed the empty glass on a nearby table. He intended to follow behind them and see what she was up to. Blake still thought there was something odd going on with the wallflowers, former and still. Though looking at Emma now, he had to wonder why she'd ever been a wallflower to begin with.

He had never paid much attention to her before. That had nothing to do with her. Blake didn't pay attention to any innocent lady searching for a husband. Especially as he didn't intend to wed. But now that he saw her, he had to appreciate what a beauty he'd found. She had golden blonde hair and striking blue eyes. Her heart-shaped face looked delicate, but those pouty lips—those were pure sin. It was like an angel come down from the heavens with the purpose of seduction. If she were not Harcrest's sister, and an innocent, he'd find out for himself if she was as wicked as she seemed. Hell, he might anyway.

Blake kept a leisurely pace as he followed them. He could hear their discussion, and he almost laughed. She played them both with ease and neither of them realized it. She strolled into the game room. At least it was empty. "Here you go, my lords," she told them. "You can play billiards in here."

"We could," they both said in unison. "But what will you do?"

"I can sit over there and watch." She had that innocent tone in her voice. "I'm not much for games. But if you need me for something, I'll still be here."

They went over to the side and grabbed cue sticks and set the game up to play. Once they started, Blake strolled into the room. "Ah," he said. "I missed a chance to play."

"You can play the winner, my lord," Emma said. She narrowed her gaze on him. Was she determining the best way to handle him, too? She would be in for a surprise.

"I'll just have a drink and watch. Not sure I

want to play." He went to the bar and poured a glass of brandy. On a whim, he poured a second glass and took it over to her.

She stared at it, then at him. "I don't…"

"Take the drink, Miss Collins," he said. "I think you have earned it."

Tentatively, she reached up and took the brandy. "And why have I earned it?" She lifted a brow.

He sat in the seat next to her. "I must say, I was surprised." Blake took a drink of his brandy. "Those two are usually not led around so easily."

She turned away from him as she said, "I'm not certain I understand your meaning."

He held out his glass toward the two men playing billiards. "They're not young fools, but you're making them out to be just that." Blake stared at her. "What is your secret?"

Emma stared at her glass of brandy and brought it up to her lips. She sipped tentatively. Blake nearly smirked, but held it back. She grimaced. "This is awful."

"But it has a nice burn," he told her. "I thought you might appreciate it." He smiled as he took another drink. It hadn't escaped his notice that she ignored his question.

She took another drink, then another. Then she

licked her lips. Blake nearly groaned. She had the best lips. He wanted to taste them and lick the brandy off those tantalizing lips. "It's growing on me," she finally said.

"It does that," he agreed. His lips curled up into a wicked smile. "Many things do."

"Why are you here?" she asked him.

"At the manor or this room?" he asked. Blake thought he might already know which, but he wanted her to be bold.

"This room," she said, then rolled her eyes. "I know why you're at the manor. I wrote all the invitations. If I didn't know you were on the guest list, I'd be a bloody fool."

That was interesting too… He hadn't realized that Lady Harcrest hadn't addressed all the invitations. "I am here," he said. "In this room to uncover what scheme you are concocting." He emptied his glass. "Because I have no doubts, there is one."

"Even if there is," she began. "It has nothing to do with you."

"That may be true," he told her. "But I'll still investigate. I don't like secrets."

She sighed. "What will it take to make you go away?"

Blake thought about it. She wouldn't let him in

on her secrets willingly. But perhaps she'd play a game with him. "How about a wager?"

"A wager?" She frowned. "What would we make a wager on?"

"I want to know what this is all about." He motioned toward the earl and viscount playing billiards. They hadn't even bothered to address him when he entered the game room. They were that focused on each other. "So, if I discover what it is you are plotting," he told her. "Then I will win."

"And if you don't—I win?" she finished.

"Exactly," he said, then grinned. "Finish your brandy, love. It is rude to waste good spirits."

She glared at him. "And if you win, what do you want from me?"

Blake only wanted one thing from her. He wanted her naked and tied to his bed, where he could pleasure her all night long. He wanted to taste every inch of her delectable skin and hear her moan with all the exquisite torture he'd deliver her. But that was asking too much. She'd never agree to it. "Why don't we make this simple," he said. "The winner will get a boon of their choosing from the winner."

"I won't allow you to seduce me," she warned.

"Sweetheart," he said. "I wouldn't need a wager

to seduce you." He leaned in close so that only she'd be able to hear him. "You'd be in my bed before you realized that you ceded everything to me." He stood. "So, do we have a wager?" He lifted a brow. "Or would you rather I take my concerns to your brother?"

"All right," she said in a resigned tone. "You have your wager."

"Excellent," he said. "I will leave you to your young bucks for now." He wiggled his eyebrows. "Happy scheming, love."

Blake left her alone in the game room. He'd find out more later. He had enough for now, and he finally had begun to enjoy this house party. All because of one little vixen that he wanted to kiss desperately, and he fully intended to at least give in to that urge before the fortnight was over.

Four

E mma had plans. Big plans. And that blasted Marquess of Ardmore was not going to interrupt them. She gnashed her teeth together in frustration. How dare he insinuate himself into her plans. She had depended upon no one noticing what she did. As a wallflower, she should have been able to depend upon that. That sneaky interfering man would rue the day he decided to pry into her activities. It didn't matter if she found him the most arrestingly gorgeous man she'd ever seen.

She had thought that Clouston and Marlinton had been attractive, and they were, however, they had nothing on the marquess. It was his eyes that did it for her. They were golden and seductive, and she could easily become lost in them. But it was more than that. He had broad shoulders, and when she was near him, she wanted to beg him to pull her into his arms. Emma had never desired a man more. But like all the gentlemen she'd ever met, the marquess hadn't noticed her. One of the most notorious rogues in the ton, and she was beneath him. Until now. Now he saw her. Right when she didn't want him to, he decided to become embroiled in her life.

It was enough to make her wonder what deity she'd angered to have fate decide to curse her. She took a deep breath and reminded herself that she had a plan. A good one. It was already in progress. She walked into the breakfast room and made sure she had a welcoming smile on her face. Her facade had to remain in place. It wouldn't do for them to look too closely at her. All of the guests she had plans for were there. Perfect.

Lord Clouston rose and approached her. He was as handsome as she remembered, but he no longer stirred anything within her. Emma held back a sigh. "Miss Collins," he greeted her. "Would you care to sit with me?"

Her first response was to say no. But he didn't. Instead, she grinned. "I would love to," she said in a friendly tone. "I see Lord Marlinton is already here as well." Emma nodded in his direction. She wanted to demand that they join him, but then Lord Clouston would realize that she was no longer following his dictates and suggestions. It had to come from him. She glanced at him and lowered her lashes submissively.

"Yes," Lord Clouston said. "He is." He smiled down at her. "Would you like me to fix you a plate?"

Emma could fix her own plate. She knew what she liked. "Of course, my lord. I'd like that." She mirrored his movements and spoke in the same tone of voice. It lulled him into compliance. The man didn't even realize that he was doing as she wished. Hmmm. All those books she'd read about this type of mind tricks were accurate so far.

"My lord," she began. "I was wondering if I could ask a favor from you."

"Of course," he said.

That easily… What if she asked him to go for a walk off the nearest cliff? What a simpleton. "Would you be a dear and give me an extra sausage?" She gestured toward her plate. "I so adore sausages."

He chuckled and put another sausage on her

plate. They moved down the buffet. She placed a hand on his arm. "My apologies, my lord." She nibbled on her bottom lip. "But would it be too much to ask if you went back for one more sausage?"

"One more?" He lifted a brow. There were already three on her plate. She really didn't like sausage that much. This was a test to see how much he would be willing to do for her. When the next part of her plan moved forward, she had to know what he might or might not do, and this was a simple request. "I do not see why not." He left her and went and retrieved another sausage for her.

"Thank you so much, my lord. You are a dear for indulging my request." She smiled as he led her over to the table. She stumbled and he reached out to help her and the plate tipped, with two of the sausages falling to the floor.

He frowned, his gaze fixed on the floor. The crestfallen look on his face was almost endearing. She should take pity on him, but she wouldn't. "Oh, dear…" She nibbled on her bottom lip. "I so wanted those sausages."

She didn't even have to make the request. The poor sod just walked away and went back to the buffet. He even put a couple of additional sausages on the plate. Perfect. He came back and set the plate down, then pulled her chair out for her. "Thank you, my lord." She would never be able to eat all the food on the plate.

"Miss Collins," Lord Marlinton greeted her. "Would you be interested in a walk in the conservatory with us later?"

Emma had something else in mind. "I thought perhaps we could do something a little more entertaining."

"Oh?" Lord Clouston said. "What would that be?"

"We had a lovely bit of snow fall overnight." That was a welcome surprise and had given her this idea. "Wouldn't it be delightful to have a snowball fight?"

"A what?" Lord Marlinton tilted his head to side.

"If a few of the gentlemen wouldn't mind making the preparations." She glanced downward. "We could divide into teams."

"Teams?" Lord Clouston said.

She sensed she was losing them. "Yes, my lord, teams. We could have...flags of some sort. The objective is to collect the other team's flag and be declared the winner."

"What would the gentlemen need to do?" Lord Marlinton asked.

"Oh, you know, create the snowballs of course. We will need to be able to act quickly and sometimes stopping to create our ammunition will be time consuming. It will be beneficial, don't you think, for us to have an armory for each team already built?"

They both stared at her as if she had lost her mind. Perhaps she had pushed them too far. Had she overplayed her hand?

"That is rather ingenious," another man said. "I'll even help build the armory." She glanced up and met the Marquess of Ardmore's gaze. "On one condition."

She was almost afraid to ask. "And what is that, my lord?"

Emma was almost terrified of what his answer would be, but she had to ask. Those golden eyes of his kept her mesmerized and she was lost to them.

BLAKE HAD NEVER BEEN MORE INTRIGUED. WHAT would this delightful wallflower gain by organizing a snowball fight, of all things? It would definitely keep the guests entertained. How would they determine the winner? Other than capturing the other team's flag, that is. There had to be rules, and he would just bet the devious minx had something specific in mind.

But that was something he'd find out soon enough. First, he had to insert himself into her little plot. How else was he to discover the master plan? "I must be on the same team as you love," he said. "I wouldn't want to break any of the rules you set."

She narrowed her gaze on him. Lord, she was lovely, especially when she wanted to say something she knew she shouldn't. Emma gritted her teeth, and then her lips tilted upward into a devastating smile. It hit him right in the gut like a punch he couldn't block. "Of course, my lord," she said in a tone that was all sweet and compliant. As if she'd do anything she asked of him. He knew better. This woman was too clever by far and would never be led around like a willing slave. That was one of the things he liked about her.

"Then it's settled," he said in a firm tone. "I'll gather some of the gentlemen," he motioned toward the two fools she'd been manipulating. "Along with those two. Once we have the armories built, we can gather the rest of the guests to form teams." He rubbed his hands together in glee. "This is going to be fun."

"What will be fun?" came the voice of a lady from across the room

Blake turned and frowned. He didn't recognize her. Hell, he didn't know any of the ladies that were looking for a husband, and he didn't want to become acquainted with this one either. This lady was a petite blonde, with bright blue eyes. She wasn't nearly as beautiful as Emma. She seemed more…cold. Emma had more fire and would be far more passionate in bed. This chit—she'd be like sleeping with a block of ice. Blake had bedded enough women to recognize that in her.

"A snowball fight," he told her. Then he smiled. She blinked at him several times. "Would you like to join us later this afternoon for the upcoming battle?"

"I don't know…" She glanced at her friend. Blake followed her gaze. This girl was taller, but much plainer. She had dull brown hair and light brown eyes—almost mousy in appearance. But she had an air about her, a haughtiness that was unmistakable. Blake didn't like her and he couldn't quite explain why. "What do you think?"

"Yes," Emma said. "What do you think, Miss Smythe?"

Interesting… Emma didn't like these two. "Please say you'll join us," he said to the two ladies.

"I suppose we can," Miss Smythe said.

"Wonderful," Emma said. She was irritated, but she hid it well. He was starting to recognize her expressions.

"Pardon me," he said. "But I don't believe we are acquainted." Blake tilted his lips into one of his wicked smiles. "I am Lord Ardmore."

"I'm aware of who you are," the lady said. She smiled back at him with interest. He'd have to stop being so charming less the chit got ideas. Ones he did not wish her to have. Blake had no interest in her. "I am Lady Arabella Jones." She batted her eyelashes at her. "My father is the Earl of Galeton."

As if that mattered. It didn't. "Is he now?" He focused on the other girl. "And you're Miss Smythe?"

"I am," she said stiffly. Ah. This one couldn't be charmed. "I *am* Miss Harriett Smythe."

"And your father is?" Blake lifted a brow. The other girl had thought it important. Why had this one not offered up the information?

"Viscount Edmonton," she said stiffly.

Ah. Her father was quite wealthy. Why was she reluctant to admit that connection? Had she been hounded by fortune hunters? Most likely. "I'm not acquainted with either of them." He knew both well, but he wouldn't admit as much. "Anyway…" He focused his attention back on Emma. "I believe me and the other gentlemen have a task to complete."

You do,' Emma replied, her glare now fixed on him. His little minx hadn't liked the attention he'd paid to the other two ladies. The more he learned, the more intrigued he became. "We will go over our rules once each fort is built properly. I look forward to the upcoming skirmish."

"I do as well." He held her gaze. Neither of them were speaking about the snowball fight. This was the battle brewing between them. So far he didn't know what she had planned, but he had a feeling he now knew who she was plotting against. Each conversation brought a little more information his way, and Blake fully intended to win their wager. He even had an idea of what he would ask from her when he won. "Until later, my lady." He bowed to her. Then he turned toward the other two gentle-men. "Shall we?"

They groaned but rose to their feet and followed

him out of the breakfast room. After a few hours outdoors, everything would be ready. Blake had some plans of his own during this snowball fight, and all of them involved getting Miss Emma Collins alone for something a little wicked.

Five

Emma strolled out to where the gentlemen had built the two separate forts for the upcoming snowball fight. At the base of each fort, a flag, or rather a ribbon, had been secured. Everyone could hide behind the stacked wood that had been built as a barricade. As for the armory… A neat pile of snowballs had been packed and formed. All the participants had to do was grab one and launch. After the preformed snowballs were depleted, then they would have to build their own.

"I think this will work," she told the marquess. "I suppose we can start picking teams."

"As long as you are on mine," he said. "By all means start your selection."

She narrowed her gaze on him. "You're enjoying this far too much, my lord."

He tilted his head to the side and studied her. "I may be, but trust me on this, I haven't nearly begun." Then he tilted his lips up into a wicked smile that did funny things to her belly. That smile made a promise. One filled with every sin imaginable, and she would like falling in with the devil that beckoned her. The marquess was a temptation she could not indulge in. Even when she desperately wanted to.

Emma shrugged. "Then I shall leave you to it." She turned toward the rest of the guests that they had convinced to participate in the snowball fight. "All right, everyone." She had an idea suddenly. It was perfect. The only problem, if one would consider it such, was the marquess would be quite irate with her. "I've decided this snowball fight is going to be more challenging. I hope that you all will appreciate how much." She grinned. "There are only a few rules. Once whichever team captures the other's flag first wins. If you're captured while attempting to retrieve the flag, you must remain in the other team's prison. There is always an opportunity to switch sides, if the other teams allows it."

"Sounds fair," Lord Clouston said. "How do we decide what teams we are on?"

"It will be simple." She grinned. "All the men will be red, and all the ladies will be green."

"What?" The marquess said. "That's not…"

She ignored him and clapped her hands. "Everyone, go to your fort and prepare for the battle. Once the bell is rung, it will begin."

Ardmore clasped her wrist. "This isn't over."

She met his gaze and tilted her lip up into a saucy smile. "Indeed, my lord. It has only just begun, as you so aptly remarked earlier." She winked. "Man, your battle station, my lord. I intend on winning."

He glared at her, but then spun on his heels to join the rest of the men. Emma had been correct. He was quite livid. But she couldn't allow him to distract her from her plans. She needed those two nitwits on her team. How else was she going to control their actions and those of the two fops she'd been cajoling to do her bidding for the past couple of days?

"All right ladies," she said with a grin. "Are you all ready to win?"

"I do not see how that is possible," Lady

Arabella said. "We're but women against men that have far superior strength than us."

She narrowed her gaze on her. "If that is how you feel, then perhaps you would like to walk over and surrender now."

Lady Arabella lifted her chin defiantly. Good. She'd done as Emma believed she would. "I do not give in. I never will."

"Then prepare to throw those snowballs." Emma motioned toward the pile. Then she turned to the rest of the women. "Arm yourselves ladies."

While they grabbed their snowballs, Emma retreated to the back. Then she rang the bell, signaling that they were to begin. Snow started to fly and mayhem ensued. Emma ducked behind the wall and took something out of her pocket. She'd hidden something special there before she'd come outside. She pulled out the slingshot and put a snowball into the small pouch. Emma peeked over the wall and surveyed everyone. Where was Ardmore? Snowballs were launched with regularity, but he was nowhere to be seen in the fray.

She could not waste any more time trying to find him. Her plan had to be set in motion. She slid behind Lady Arabella and then selected her target. The snowball flew through the air and hit Lord Marlinton in the face. It splatted perfectly. She knelt down and loaded the slingshot again. This time she got behind Miss Harriett Smythe, then launched again. This time it hit Lord Clouston. Splendid. Both men reacted how she'd expected. They turned their attention to the ladies. Good. Lady Arabella had set her cap for Lord Marlinton. She was just helping them along. Harriett had fallen for Clouston, but he never noticed her. Well, he did not, and definitely not in the way she had hoped. The look on her face when he threw that snowball at her. Nothing would ever compare to that.

Emma circled back and considered the next place to send a snowball. She never got a chance to launch it. She was pulled back against something warm and solid. "Hello, love," he said and he wrapped his arms around her. He put a hand over her mouth and dragged her away from the fort. "Time to join me and the others. You are my prisoner now."

Drat. He had taken the part about capturing prisoners to heart. At least she'd gotten off two volleys before he'd done his own form of damage. Her plan was still in place. Emma didn't really care who won the battle. She'd already won hers.

Ardmore didn't take her back to the fort as she

had thought he would. Instead, he took her into the woods and away from the snowballs still flying through the air. He spun her around and pinned her against a tree. "Now," he said, as he trailed a finger over her jawline. "that I have your attention. You owe me a forfeit."

"I do not," she glared at him.

"You do," he said. "You agreed that we would be on the same team. Then you went and changed the rules as though there would be no consequences. There are, and you're about to find out exactly what they are."

BLAKE HAD NEVER BEEN SO ANGRY AND AROUSED AT the same time in his life. What was it about this woman that drove him to do things he normally would never have considered? He wanted her. Desperately. What the bloody hell was wrong with him?

All he knew was he had to kiss her. It was a driving need in him that he couldn't ignore. Just one little kiss and once he had slaked his need, he could walk away from her. It would be enough. It had to be enough.

She pushed at him. "Let me go."

"Not yet, love," he told her.

He grasped her wrists in one hand and lifted them above her head. She wiggled against him and he groaned. His cock hardened almost painfully. The little minx had him acting like a young cub, about to get a taste of his first woman. He had to slow down, seduce her. Somehow, he would find his finesse and give Emma pleasure. Because only with her pleasure could he find his own. Blake prided himself on never being selfish with women.

He lowered his head and brushed his lips over hers. Gentle, coaxing, and sweet… He forgot everything around him. The cold disappeared. It was just her and him, and this moment. Blake licked at her lips until she opened for him. Then he pushed his tongue inside and tasted heaven. He moaned and deepened the kiss. Emma was all in with him. Her passion overtook her as she brushed her tongue over his. They were lost in that kiss, and he could have her. He wanted her. But he would not take her. Not like this out here in the cold. But, oh, he wanted to. It would be so easy to lift her skirts and take her against the tree.

Somehow, he found the strength to pull away. His breathing was heavy, and she panted just as hard. Her lips were plump and her cheeks red. He doubted that had been from the cold. Her blonde hair had come undone. He didn't even remember mussing it. She had never looked more beautiful. He let her hands go. Emma stumbled and almost fell, but he caught her in his arms. Blake was tempted to kiss her again.

"I suppose that was my forfeit," she said. Her tone was husky and reminded him of a well pleasured woman. What would she sound like after she climaxed? He would bet it would be even more arousing to hear her then.

"Perhaps," he said. "I have not decided." Blake didn't know what he was going to do from one moment to the next. His every waking thought had been consumed by him. She had even started to haunt his dreams. He didn't know what hold she had over him, but he didn't like it.

"How about I decide for you, then?" She lifted her hands and pressed them on his chest. Emma didn't push him away as he had expected her to. Instead, she lifted her hands and pushed them through his hair, then grabbed on to them and yanked his head forward. She pressed her lips to his, then slid her tongue into his mouth. She had learned what he liked quickly and used it to her advantage. Blake was once again lost to her.

He slid his hand up to cup her breast. If she wanted to play with fire, then he'd ensure she burned. He tweaked one of her nipples, and she moaned into him. Blake took off his glove. He had to feel her flesh beneath his fingers. He pulled at her skirts and slid his fingers over her things. Blake pressed his knee between her legs and spread them for him. Then he found her core and started to stroke as he kissed her.

Emma squirmed beneath him. She was close. He lowered his head and sucked one of her earlobes into his mouth. Her gasps grew louder as he stroked her. When she reached her peak, she opened her mouth to scream. Blake covered her mouth with his and swallowed her cries. They didn't need the other guests to hear her reach her pleasure.

He had thought her beautiful after a kiss, but this… It was so breathtaking he almost forgot how to draw air into his lungs. He gasped for breath. His cock was still so hard that he never thought he'd know any other feeling. If they were in any other place, he might have taken her innocence. Blake wanted to make her his, but that was impossible. He wasn't the marrying kind and she deserved so much more than he could ever give her.

Pleasure, he could easily offer her, but nothing else. He wished he were a better man, but he never would be, never could be, anything other than what he was—a rogue, a scoundrel, a consummate rake.

"We should go back inside. I think the battle has been won."

Her lips twitched. "Yours or the snowball fight?"

He grinned at her. "Can't it be both?" She was still so utterly beautiful.

She shrugged. "You may have won this time, my lord, but I promise, I'll prevail in our next skirmish."

He closed his eyes and groaned. Blake suddenly had the image of her riding him as she climaxed, and he desperately wanted to have that. Life was cruel because she could never truly be his. He put his gloves back on and led her out of the woods. They had to get back inside. Blake needed distance from her and the sooner, the better. It was time that he left her alone. Because if he spent any more time with her, he would have her, and that would be disastrous.

Six

Emma strolled into the conservatory to grab some supplies. To be more specific, the mistletoe she'd had the gardener grow for her. It hadn't been done specifically for this house party. Emma had requested it be grown years earlier. Back when she had romantic notions and believed she would one day fall in love. How naïve she had been. She knew better now. Love was for the lucky few that managed to find it. Emma had never been that fortunate, and had doubts she ever would be.

Passion though… That was possible. She had found that out rather abruptly the day before. Never would she have imagined she would find it in the arms of the Marquess of Ardmore. The things she had allowed him to do to her… She closed her eyes and muffled a groan remembering how he'd touched her—how she longed for him to caress her again. Emma wanted him. Almost desperately. The way he had kissed her had left her nearly mindless. The desire he had stoked within her had left her reeling. She wanted him then. Would have allowed him to take her innocence. A part of her still did, even away from his mind-numbing kisses.

She gathered the mistletoe and headed to the library. There were several places that she wanted to hang the mistletoe throughout the house. Emma had plans for the mistletoe. The snowball fight had served its purpose. The two ladies and gentlemen, she had targeted, continued to glare at each other. The next step was to have one gentleman kiss one of the ladies—but not the one that the lady in question preferred. That would only ensure the continued discord between them. With the added benefit of creating animosity between the two ladies. By the time they all left there would be a stream of loathing all around.

In the library, she found the ladder that she had asked a servant to bring into the room. She wanted to hang the mistletoe in a few places, but in the library, she needed something to climb. She arranged the mistletoe on a long red velvet ribbon, and then settled the ladder over the part of the ceiling where she wanted it hung. Emma climbed up and then tied the ribbon over a hook that was already embedded in the ceiling.

"Don't you have servants that can do that for you?" Ardmore asked.

The sound of his voice startled her and she lost her balance. Fear spiked through her and her heart began to beat rapidly. She flailed her arms in an attempt to stop her impending fall. Her efforts were not successful. Her foot slipped and then she plummeted toward the floor. She never hit the ground. Instead, Ardmore's warm arms wound around her and he held her close to him. Her breathing was ragged and her heart continued to race.

"Are you all right?" he asked.

She shoved at his chest. "Put me down."

"You're welcome, love," he drawled. "Not that you bothered to say thank you."

"I wouldn't have fallen if you hadn't startled me," she told him. Emma knew she sounded churlish but damn him. She had been fine until he sneaked up on her. "Now put me down," she ordered him again.

"I don't think I will," he said. "I like having you in my arms. It's much easier to keep you from doing something foolish."

Emma gritted her teeth. Ardmore was insufferable and she wanted to hit him. Perhaps she should. She considered it for a brief moment but held back. Violence never solved anything. Revenge however was always a possibility. She could make him pay for his misdeeds in a much cleverer way. "I do not need your assistance with anything, my lord. You are nothing to me. Why are you even bothering to follow me around to ascertain what my activities are? Please explain to me why you care."

"You intrigue me," he said. Then he smiled at her. That tilt of his lips that warned any female with clear vision that he had wicked intentions. She had to get him to set her down so she could put some distance between them. Emma did not need him to explore the building passion between them. That would be disastrous. She might even beg him for more. Hell, she was tempted to do that regardless. "And I still have not uncovered your master plan."

"You do not need to know that." She sighed. "It

has nothing to do with you." Emma needed him to go find some other mystery to occupy himself with. She would not be able to finish her plans if he insisted on inserting himself into everything she did. "Just leave me be. Is that too much to ask?"

"Yes," he said. "Three of my friends have attended house parties and fallen in love. They are all blissfully happy, and that disturbs me."

"Let me see if I understand this," she began. The audacity of this man… He still held her in his arms as if she weighed nothing. "Three of your friends are now happily married and because they found that love at a house party, you are disturbed?" She rolled her eyes. "I can promise, my lord, that as far as I'm aware, no woman here has designs on you. If you fear marriage and love, you may rest assured—you are quite safe."

He narrowed his gaze. "I never said that I was worried about that."

"You didn't need to," she said. "Now can you please let me down? There is no reason for you to continue to hold me."

"I beg to differ." He flashed her that sinful grin again and she almost caved and begged him to give her pleasure again. "There is one very good reason for me to keep you in my arms."

"Your reasons are senseless," she nearly whined.

"Not this one." He gestured to the ceiling. "We have to honor the tradition, don't we?"

She glanced up at the ceiling and groaned. They were directly under the mistletoe that she had just hung, and the rogue intended to take advantage of it. The sad part—Emma didn't blame him. If she were in his shoes, she'd have done the same, and to make it worse—she wanted him to.

BLAKE KNEW HE SHOULDN'T BE DOING THIS. Especially after he had pleasured her in the forest the day before. That had been beyond foolish. He had lifted her skirts in the frigid weather and stroked her until she climaxed. That passion he'd tasted on her lips had been like nothing he'd ever felt. He wanted to experience it again. Surely it couldn't be that good again. It had to be all in his imagination.

He lowered his head and pressed his lips to hers. The first taste was his own version of ambrosia. Decadent and consuming. A taste that he would never be able to forget. He held her against him and he plundered her mouth. Desire heated his blood and the temptation to walk her out of the library and straight up to his bedchamber filled his every thought. He wanted to strip the gown off of her body and worship her with his tongue.

Her moans only encouraged him to continue to savor her. He lowered his head and trailed kisses around her neck, then kissed up until he reached her ear. "You're so lovely," he whispered in his ear. "I could kiss you over and over again. I'd like to do more than that. I want to taste all of you."

"No," she said huskily. "You can't."

"I could," he said. "Just say yes. I promise you pleasure that you'll never forget."

She shook her head. "I don't doubt that. But it would be a mistake, my lord."

"Blake," he said. "No more my lord, or formal titles. I am Blake. Say my name."

"That's not wise either." She sighed. "We cannot do this. This will ruin me if even one person walks into the library. You need to put me down."

Blake didn't want to agree with her. He wanted to continue to persuade her that she would love for him to pleasure her. His desire for her was consuming him beyond all ability to reason. He wanted her and the lure of her beauty and taste… Damn it all. Blake inhaled sharply as he did his best to regain control. He took a few more deep breaths, then set her down.

She slid against him until her feet touched the floor. It was equal parts agony and ecstasy. Blake had every intention of letting her go, but he had to taste her one last time. He lowered his head and brushed his lips over hers. A light press of his lips that shouldn't have stirred his blood. He should have known better, though. Everything about her made him run hot. He slid his hand over her waist and pulled her against him. Blake deepened the kiss and slid his tongue against hers.

The day before he had brought her to climax. He was tempted to do that again, but he couldn't. She had made a valid argument against their continued passion. Just by kissing her this way, he had compromised her, but no one had witnessed it. They both could deny he had ever touched her or kissed her. But the moment they were caught, there would be no turning back.

Slowly, Blake let go of her and stepped back. Emma drew in some shallow breaths. Her lips were plump from his kiss and her eyes were a little glazed. "You should not have kissed me," she told him. She brought her hand up and touched her lips tentatively. "It was a mistake."

"I do not make mistakes," he said. "That would imply I have something to regret." He leaned in and whispered, "Remorse is the last thing I feel when I think of how you felt in my arms."

"You are wicked," she said breathlessly.

"But you like it." He tilted her lips up into a sinful smile. "And you like me. Admit it."

Blake didn't know why he was insisting on this. Did it matter how she felt about him? He didn't even understand his own feelings regarding Emma. She meant something to him. But what exactly he felt—he couldn't answer that. A part of him wanted to explore it and uncover the deeper meaning of it all. He wouldn't, though. Because he wasn't prepared for the answers.

"I never disliked you." She rolled her eyes. "But you *are* a nuisance. One I do not need right now. So, if you would kindly leave me be, I'd appreciate it."

"I might consider it," he said. "If you answer one question."

There were several things he wanted to know about her. She didn't know it yet, but she wasn't going to get her way. He had every intention of seeing this wager through. For some reason, he had to know what she was up to and why. Emma fascinated him.

"And what would that be?"

"What do you have against Lady Arabella and Miss Harriett?"

She glanced away from him. He'd been correct. Something about that snowball fight had to do with those two women. What had they done to her? Emma didn't seem like the spiteful type of lady. If she was scheming against them, then she had a reason for it. He just didn't know what it was.

"They're perfectly respectable ladies," she said. "I don't have any difficulties with them."

He leaned in and said, "Liar."

"Believe what you will," she said defiantly. "I don't owe you any explanations."

Blake grinned. "Then you can count on me following you around until I discover everything." He winked. "I must thank you for continuing to make this house party inherently more interesting. I so feared I'd be bored."

"I do not do anything with your entertainment in mind." She glared at him. "And from this moment on." Her tone was irate as she ground out the words "You had best be prepare for disappointment."

Emma turned and left him alone in the library. He allowed her to leave because he doubted that she had any nefarious plans. At least not yet. She still had some mistletoe to hang and he had a sneaky suspicion that nothing would happen until sometime after she finished. That gave him some time to make some plans of his own.

Seven

Emma sat at her vanity as her maid secured her golden hair up in a Grecian style. Large voluminous plaits were secured at the sides and secured with seed pearl pins with her remaining locks left in loose curls flowing down her back. A few of those curling locks were secured up against the plaits to make it messy, but more uniform. The entire hairstyle had a romantic appearance. Once the maid was finished placing a few strategic seed pearl pins into her blond hair, she took thThe diadem was finely crafted gold, shaped like leaves, accented by pearls and rubies that set into her hair like a band.

"It's lovely," her maid said, then sighed. "You look beautiful tonight."

Her gown was as red as the rubies in her diadem and trimmed with white lace that resembled the finely crafted leaves. The leaves were the same shape as the mistletoe she'd hung around the manor, the day before. Tonight was the masquerade ball she'd planned for the eve before Christmas. She wanted something different for this house party. The requirement of masks would make her tasks so much easier. All she had to do was lure her prey to the mistletoe so one man would kiss the wrong woman. Not that the gentleman in question would understand their error, but the women would.

The only thing left was for her to secure her mask in place. It was red lace, similar to the lace on her gown. She had her entire outfit for the evening decided especially for the masquerade. The modiste had been enthusiastic about her requests and had outdone herself. It was all perfect. Emma placed the mask on her face and tied the ribbon at the back of her head, and tucked it into the loose curls there to hide it from view.

Emma felt decadent. The silk of her gown brushed against her skin leaving her warm all over. Ever since Blake had kissed her, and introduced her to pleasure, she'd been unable to think of anything else. Her entire body would come alive at the most inopportune times. Right now she her nipples pebbled as need scorched through her. The desire to seek him out and beg for his touch overwhelmed her. It was enough to make her hate him for what he had awakened within her. It made her revenge scheme harder to focus on. She wanted him and what he could do for her. Somehow she had to suppress the urges that rippled within her. This was the final night, and at the end of it, she'd know the satisfaction of destroying something for those two women. They would understand what it felt like to be slighted, and they would have a wedge inserted into their seemingly unbreakable friendship.

She stood and slipped on the red slippers that matched her gown. They were pretty, but not the most comfortable shoes she'd ever owned. Since they matched so perfectly, though she'd endure a little pain. Emma didn't usually follow fashion or care much about how pieces went together. This was a special night and she wanted it all to be perfect, and it would be. Emma intended to ensure it. One way or the other…

It was time to go down to the ballroom. Since it was a masquerade, there would be no formal announcements of any of the guests. The local gentry had been invited as well. This would be a true Christmastide celebration. Holly had been strung along the walls, and mistletoe had been placed at every entrance and a few other strategic places. It was those places she wanted to lure her quarries to.

Emma slipped into the ballroom by a side entrance. The room was bathed in low light from a few scattering candles that had been lit in wall sconces. The musicians had begun to play for those who wished to dance. They were playing a lively quadrille that was near the end of the song. With masks, it would take her a little longer to find Lady Arabella. She needed to lure her under that mistletoe at the same time as Lord Clouston. She wanted Lord Marlinton so the viscount would have to be the one to kiss her. Equally as important, Miss Harriett had to witness that kiss.

As she wound her way through the crowd, she searched first for Arabella. She had to be under any of the mistletoe, but she would prefer a specific one. Finally, she found the lady she'd been searching for. Emma had to handle this carefully to get the outcome she desired. Emma pretended that she did not see Arabella and bumped into her. She glanced up and said, "My apologies…"

"You clumsy fool," Arabella scowled at her. "You made me spill punch all over my gown."

She nibbled on her lip. "I did try to apologize."

"Now I have to go to the retiring room and see if my gown can be salvaged." She glared at Emma. "Go bother someone else with your ungainly movements." Arabella stalked off in the direction that Emma had hoped. When she returned, she would be easily waylaid under a particular bunch of mistletoe."

Now to take care of the other woman. She forced herself to move slowly toward Miss Harriett Smythe. She was staring up at Lord Clouston adoringly. Emma barely refrained from rolling her eyes. She stopped and frowned. "Miss Harriett?"

She turned toward Emma. "Yes?" Her gown was a deep blue and her mask a simple white. She hadn't done much to dress for the masquerade.

"Why is that you, Miss Emma?" Clouston asked.

"Lord Clouston," she said as she curtsied. "Indeed, it is."

"What do you want?" Harriett demanded.

"Pardon my interruption," she told them as she laid a hand on the viscount's arm. "But I was asked to give you a message, Miss Harriett. Lady Arabella requires your assistance. She had to return to her bedchamber." That should keep her out of the ballroom long enough to put the rest of the plan into place.

"Then I must see to her," Harriett said. She turned to Lord Clouston. "Pardon me, my lord." She curtsied and rushed out of the ballroom, in the opposite direction of the retiring room. So far, everything was going as planned. Now just to lead Clouston to the finale.

"Would you give me the honor of escorting you out for the next dance?" he asked.

He wanted to dance with her. She frowned, but what would it hurt? She could talk to him while they joined the next quadrille, and after he could find Arabella under that mistletoe. "Of course," she said and held out her hand to him. They went out to the floor for the quadrille. They lined up with three other couples for the dance and begun. When she met with Lord Clouston, "Thank you for asking me to dance."

"It's my pleasure," he told her. He might even mean that.

They continued on through the steps. By the end of this dance, the viscount had to be heading toward the mistletoe. Finally, the last strands of the song wound. Lord Clouston led her off the dance floor. "My, I am parched. I must go in search of some punch."

"I can retrieve a glass for you," he offered.

"Do not trouble yourself, my lord." She smiled at him. "If you wish to be of assistance, please go see how Lady Arabella fares." She motioned toward Arabella, who was drawing close to where Emma wanted her. She just needed Clouston there as well.

He stared at where Arabella was walking. "Are you certain?"

"I am," she said. "Oh, and Lord Clouston."

"Yes?" he asked.

"It's a masquerade. Have fun." She winked. "And do take advantage of the mistletoe. It's hanging for a reason."

His cheeked pinkened a little bit. "I'll consider it."

She prayed he did more than consider it. Emma turned away from him and headed toward the punch table. She peeked over her shoulder, and her grin widened. That timing could not have happened better. Just as Arabella stepped under the mistletoe, Lord Clouston joined her. Then the magic of mistletoe did her work for her. He leaned down and pressed his lips to Arabella's for a brief kiss just as Miss Harriett returned to the ballroom. She stared at Lord Clouston and Arabella, then fled the ballroom again. Well, that was interesting. She had thought that Harriett would have confronted her friend. Perhaps that part would come later.

BLAKE STUDIED EMMA AS SHE MADE HER ROUNDS IN the ballroom. Had she known how sinful she'd look in that brilliant red gown? He wanted to unwrap her slowly, and taste every inch of the gift she had presented to him. His desire for her grew from moment to moment, and the kisses and pleasure they had already shared had only made him frenzied. What was it about her that drove him mad?

Then she went and danced that quadrille with the fop she'd been flirting with. Well, one of them anyway. He couldn't recall which was which. Not that it mattered. The fact that she seemed to have some scheme planned where they were concerned did. So, he stayed in the shadows and observed everything. Even that blasted dance where he had to grit his teeth the entire time.

He narrowed his gaze as she moved away from the dance floor. She parted ways with the gentleman and he… Blake frowned and tilted his head. Was that Lady Arabella he walked toward? How interesting. Lady Arabella stopped right under a spring of mistletoe. All that mistletoe that Emma had hung in every nook and cranny of the manor. Was this her plan? To get some of the guests to kiss openly? Did she honestly think a masquerade ball was enough to hide identities so no one would be compromised?

Or maybe that was what she had wanted all along. Had she hoped that Lady Arabella would be ruined? Why? He left his hiding place and stalked toward her. It was time for her to fess up and tell him the truth. There had to be a reason for all of this secrecy and deception. He caught up with Emma as she was about to exit the ballroom. Perfect. He slid his arm around her waist and led her in the direction he wanted her to go.

"Unhand me," she ordered.

"Not yet, love," he drawled. "I can't have you running off when we have much to discuss."

She shoved at him, but he kept a grip around

her. Once they were out of sight from anyone who might witness it, he lifted her into his arms and carried her. She still struggled, but it was far more manageable this way.

"Blake," she gritted out. "I am not a sack of grains for you to haul around. I demand you put me down. Now."

"I am pleased you remembered to use my given name, darling," he said in an amused tone. "But that's not enough for me to give in to any demands you feel like throwing at me."

"You're an insufferable lout," she ground out vehemently. "Why are you doing this?"

"All in good time," he said cheerfully.

Blake was enjoying this. Far too much… He liked having her in his arms. There was something about her. He'd been drawn to her from the moment he'd arrived at this house party. Now he couldn't stay away from her. He was done fighting it.

He carried her into the sitting room at the back of the house, a good distance from the ballroom. Blake shut the door and turned the lock before he set her down. She shoved him against the door and stepped back, glaring at him. The candlelight was low in this room, much like the other rooms for the masquerade.

"Why did you bring me in here?" she asked. "I don't want to be here with you."

He leaned against the door and folded his arms across his chest, then he tilted his lips up into a sly smile. Blake had her locked in the room with him. Now that he had her there, he could take his time. They had all night to explore what was between them until they both had the truth. He needed to understand her, and what it was he felt for her. He'd never experienced anything like this with any other woman. Emma was special. He couldn't explain it, but he knew that deep down in his soul.

"Yes, you do, love," he told her. "You want to be with me as much as I do you."

"No, I don't," she said in a belligerent tone. "Now move away from the door, so I may leave."

"I'm afraid I cannot allow that," he told her in a firm tone. "We're not done yet."

Blake still had a lot more to do with her, but first, he had some questions. "What did you do with Lady Arabella and that coxcomb you were dancing with?"

She furrowed her eyebrows. "Do you mean Lord Clouston?"

"If that's his name," he said in a cool tone. "Then yes."

Emma shrugged. "We danced. There was no grand scheme in that. Many of the guests were dancing." She met his gaze. "That is usually what one does at a ball, or has it been so long since you have attended one that you've forgotten that basic aspect?"

He lifted a brow. "That's not what I meant, darling." Blake pushed off of the door and stalked toward her. "You're deflecting. That little kiss between them under the mistletoe." He moved a step closer. "You orchestrated that. Why?"

"The mistletoe is everywhere," she said. "I had the servants hand more after that little incident where I ended up in your arms. It's supposed to be all in good fun."

"Until it isn't," Blake said.

She was still keeping secrets. What would it take for her to admit what she'd done? Blake wanted answers, but he was also tired of it all. There was something he wanted far more than the truth. He wanted her. It was as simple as that. He closed the distance between them until he stood in front of her.

"What are you doing?" she asked. It came out

breathy, as if she anticipated exactly what he planned.

He reached up and stroked a finger over her jawline. Then he slid his hand to her neck and up into her soft blond curls. Her hairstyle tonight was one of the things that had driven him mad. He wanted to pull out those pins and let her curls loose. Blake wanted to muss her and leave his mark on her. One that she would never forget. He reached underneath her hair and tugged on the ribbon that secured that red lace mask on her face and freed it.

"That's better," he said.

"What about your mask?" she asked.

"Remove it if it bothers you," he ordered.

So she did. He grinned down at her before he lowered his head to capture her lips with his. The kiss seared his soul. Every time they came together like this, he gave another piece of himself over to her care. He brought her flush against him and slid his hand down to cup her waist. She pulled back and stared at him. She licked her lips and he groaned.

"We can't keep doing this," she said.

"I must disagree," he said. "We definitely should do this, and often." Blake should have taken her to his bedchamber. Then he could have stripped that gown from her slowly, as he'd imagined since the first moment he'd laid eyes upon her that night. He brushed his lips over her jaw and then drew her ear into his mouth and sucked. "You want this. I want you."

She sucked in a breath. "We shouldn't…"

"Tell me to let you go," he said. "Say you don't want me and I'll walk away." It would kill him, but he would do it. As much as he desired her, he wouldn't push her into something she wasn't ready for. They would find their way back to each other. He firmly believed that. If he had to, he could wait for her, and he would. Because he suddenly understood something he hadn't recognized before this moment. That feeling he couldn't identify—it was simple. He loved her. Her clever mind and beautiful face had pulled at him. Why he'd never seen her before, he couldn't know. But he did now, and he wanted forever with her.

"No," she told him. Then she cupped his cheek. "Don't go. Stay here with me. Be with me."

He leaned down and pressed his forehead to hers. "Be sure this is what you want."

"I am," she told him. "Kiss me, Blake."

He didn't need her to tell him again. Blake rained kisses over her face. She sighed and then grabbed onto his waistcoat and yanked him forward. He understood. His desperation for her had heightened. They began to remove clothing as fast as possible. When she stood before him in just a shift, and him in his breeches, they stopped. Just long enough to take each other in. Then he carried her over to the settee and set her down. He kneeled before her and removed her slippers, then reached beneath her shift and untied her garter, slowly peeled off her stocking, then repeated the process with the other one.

"You're skin is so soft," he said. Before he pushed her back on the settee and spread her thighs. He leaned in and kissed her thigh, then pressed a kiss to her core. She moaned, but once he began to stroke his tongue over that tight bud, she writhed beneath him.

"Blake," she moaned his name. "More."

And that would be his pleasure. He slid a finger inside her as he sucked her sensitive nub. One more lick, followed by a stroke, and then she peaked. God, she was beautiful when she climaxed. He'd never tire of that sight.

He pushed up her shift and removed it. She was gloriously naked now. Blake pulled off his breeches and joined her on the settee. He continued to stroke her and lowered his head to suck one of her pert nipples into his mouth.

"You're destroying me," she said huskily.

"No more than you are me," he told her. He sucked on her nipple as he tweaked the other between his thumb and forefinger. She was his own little slice of heaven. "I need to be inside of you."

"Yes," she said. "I want you."

He might be going to hell for this, but he had to have her. Blake settled between her thighs and settled at her entrance. He had to make this good for her, or as good as possible, considering her innocence. To distract her, he kissed her as he entered her. He continued to slide his tongue against hers as he pressed inside of her until he was completely seated. She gasped as he pushed all the way in and he stopped. "Are you all right?" he asked.

She nodded. "Yes," Emma said. "Love me, Blake."

"Always," he whispered. Then he began to move. He slid out of her, and then slowly back in. She wrapped her legs around his waist, drawing him deeper inside. Blake kept the slow pace until she began to moan again. Emma was close to reaching her peak again. When she crested, it sent him over the edge until he spilled inside of her.

Everything went black as he climaxed. Nothing had ever felt so intense and consuming. He rolled them to the side and he held her as she curled against him. It was something he'd never forget. Loving her changed something inside of him. Now he just had to convince her that this was where she belonged.

# Eight

Emma soaked in a warm bath. Her body had aches in places she didn't realize could ache, and she also felt deliciously loved. The night with Blake had been beyond anything she could have dreamt. He'd had her in more ways than one, and her imagination would never have come up with all of them. Perhaps having a rogue as her first lover had been a most inspired choice. Not that she had been thinking about any of that when she begged him to take her. It had been desire and need driving her when she was in his arms.

Leaving him to return to her bedchamber had been difficult. She hadn't wanted to be parted from him. Something had changed between them. Emma wasn't certain she wanted to define it yet. Their connection was tenuous and fragile. What if something destroyed it? She wasn't certain she would be able to survive that devastation. Emma had never truly felt happiness. Every bit she had, she'd had to fight for in order to keep that small amount.

She closed her eyes and reminded herself to breathe. It was best not to beg for trouble that had not reared its ugly head. Blake hadn't made any promises, but he hadn't spurned her either. He may very well want the same things she did. The only way she was to discern any of it was to have an actual conversation with him. Speculation would not aid her in this. Only the truth would, and for that she'd need to seek out Blake. The sooner the better.

After she finished her bath, she rang for her maid. She had to dress as quickly as possible and seek him out. It was Christmas Day and there would be a big luncheon for all of the guests. They had some holiday entertainments planned as well. She couldn't make herself care about any of it. Not even the results of her revenge scheme. None of it mattered compared to her newfound feelings for Blake.

Her maid came into the room. 'Good morning,' she said. 'Do you need help to dress?

"Yes," she replied. "I want to wear the blue day gown. Can you dress my hair in a similar fashion as you did for the masquerade?"

"Of course," her maid answered.

Her maid helped her dress and then she sat at her vanity. The gentle pull of the brush through her hair relaxed her. She drifted back to the night before and the pleasure she found with Blake. The way that man kissed. A shiver rolled up her spine as she the sensual memory poured over her. She couldn't wait to feel his lips on hers again. She closed her eyes and imagined that reunion. It was so decadent and enthralling she remained in the fantasy the entire time that her maid dressed her hair.

"All done," her maid announced.

Her eyelids fluttered open and she smiled. "Thank you. That will be all." She could finish preparing for her meeting with Blake on her own. Her maid curtsied and left the room.

Emma sat and slid on her boots. She wanted to be comfortable and slippers usually pinched her toes. After she was satisfied with her appearance, she left her bedchamber and went in search of

Blake. She strolled into the drawing room hoping he'd be there, but not really expecting him to be. The drawing room wasn't his usual haunt.

She stopped short when she entered. Blake wasn't there, but some guests were. The very guests she'd invited for purposes of revenge. Lady Arabella Jones and Miss Harriett Smythe stood facing each other. Now this was interesting… Perhaps finding Blake could wait a few moments longer after all.

"You know how I feel about him," Harriett said in a cold tone. Her anger wasn't the sort that burned bright, but turned to ice. Emma would never have guessed that. "You should have stopped him from kissing you."

Arabella rolled her eyes. "There is no need to be so dramatic." She sighed. "It was a kiss under the mistletoe. It meant nothing."

"Then why permit it at all? I thought you were my friend." She glared at Arabella. "Friends do not betray each other."

"Get over your self-importance." Arabella stomped her food. "You know better. I don't have friends. What I have is people that are useful to me. Perhaps your relevance as one of my attendants has come to an end."

"I am not a servant, Arabella." Harriett shoved

her. Arabella flailed as she tried to remain upright, but she lost that battle and crashed to the floor. "I may have been wrong about you, but mistakes can be rectified. You are as unimportant to me as you found me. Do not bother to seek me out again. You're no longer welcome in my life."

"That's perfectly acceptable to me," Arabella sat up on the floor. "As I no longer wish to have you in my life as well."

This had been what she'd hoped for. They had taken her roommate away from her. At the time Fenella had been her only friend. Now they would understand that loss. At least she knew Fenella had survived her near drowning and gone home. Emma had just never had any contact with her again.

"Emma," someone said from behind her.

She turned and blinked. Emma should have recognized her voice, but she hadn't paid enough attention when she'd heard her name. All her focus had been on the argument between Arabella and Harriett. She lifted a hand to her chest and gasped, "Fenella?"

Emma had invited Fenella, but she hadn't expected her to attend. She never responded to any letters she sent. Why would she accept an invitation to attend a Christmastide house party? She had sent it more out of a habit than with any anticipation of her showing. But here she was, in front of her.

"Hello, Emma," she said in a soft tone. "My apologies for arriving so late." Her hair was still a bright red, and those green eyes of hers remained arresting. Her freckles had lessened, but some still scattered across her nose and cheeks. It was endearing. "We ran into a spot of trouble on our way here."

A man walked in and nodded. "Are you all right, my dear?"

She smiled at him. It was an older gentleman. He had some silver in his dark hair, and green eyes the same shade as Fenella's. "Father, she said. This is Miss Emma Collins. My dearest friend." She turned to Emma. "This is my father, The Earl of Mar."

"Lord Mar," Emma nodded at him. "I' am glad you were both able to attend. We still have a few days left of Christmastide, and you're most welcome." Far more welcome that the two women she'd been staring at before Fenella's arrival.

Fenella glanced at them now. "Why are they here?"

"Ending their friendship, apparently." Emma

held back a grin. Best not to be smug and let them know how they'd ended up having a disagreement.

Harriett nodded at them. "Hello, Lady Fenella," she said. Harriett stepped forward. "I am glad you're here. I owe you a long overdue apology. All those years ago…" She drew in a breath. "I allowed myself to be led down a dangerous path, and that almost led to you losing far too much. I regret what happened, and I'm grateful that Emma was able to save you that day. I don't expect forgiveness, but I am offering you my apologies, nonetheless."

"Thank you," Fenella said. "I am grateful for that."

Arabella said nothing. She pushed past them and left the drawing room. Emma shook her head. Of course Arabella would not apologize. She never believed herself in the wrong. "Please come in," she told Lord Mar and Fenella. "I'll order tea."

"That would be lovely," Fenella said. "But I'm tired and wish to rest. We can have tea this after-noon. I've missed you."

"All right," Emma said. "Go rest. We have time later to talk."

Fenella hugged Emma, then she left the drawing room. Her father followed behind her. Lord Mar seemed overprotective, but Emma didn't blame him for having caution where Fenella was concerned. She had almost died. If she had a child that nearly perished, then she'd want to keep them safe as well.

That left her alone with Harriett. She turned toward her. "That was kind of you to apologize."

She sighed. "It was long overdue. That day…" She glanced away. "We were reckless, and Fenella almost paid the price for it. She was owed more than an apology."

Emma agreed, but she had not thought Harriett would have believed as much. She decided to take pity on Harriett. She seemed much kinder than Arabella. "I overheard your disagreement," she began. "It's not my place to comment on your difficulties. But I would like to say one thing. Lord Clouston is a kind man. You shouldn't be too upset with him. I did hang mistletoe all over the manor."

"You may be correct," she said softly. "But I'm not ready to accept it." Harriett's eyes were filled with pain. Emma had done that to her. "I need time to grieve what I've lost. Arabella was my closest friend. I knew she could be cruel, but I never thought she'd be that way with me." She smiled, but it did not reach her eyes. "If you'll pardon me, I am going to rest in my chambers. If you don't mind, I may join you and Lady Fenella for afternoon tea."

"That would be all right with me." She thought Fenella would agree as well. "Go rest if that is what you need."

Harriett left the drawing room. Emma moved to the window and stared out at the stark white landscape. She was alone now and left with her thoughts. She still had to locate Blake and have a conversation with him, as well. The morning had been enlightening. Her revenge had been far more successful that she had thought it would be. How would Arabella have reacted if Lord Marlinton had kissed Harriett? She would have been far more vicious. It was fortunate that her opportunity hadn't been in the reverse. Emma feared what Arabella might have done.

"There you are," Blake said. "I have been searching for you."

She turned and met his gaze. Emma grinned. "I've been here for a while now. Where have you looked?"

"Well," he said. "I did start at your bedchamber. I must confess I had hoped to find you still in your bed." He walked toward her and pulled her into his arms. "I wanted to join you there." Blake pressed a quick kiss to her lips. "I missed you."

"Did you?" Happiness filled her. "Then it's

unfortunate that I did not stay in bed." She wrapped her arms around his neck. "I would have welcomed you." She stepped on her tiptoes and whispered. "It's also sad that you missed joining me in my bedchamber as I bathed. That was quite the missed opportunity."

He groaned. "You're a minx." Blake brushed the back of his hand over her cheek. "But you're mine." His eyes were warm and not just from the desire he clearly felt for him. "Emma, love," he began. "We have much to discuss."

"We do," she agreed. "We were too busy last night to say much of anything."

Blake lifted her into his arms and carried her over to the settee. He didn't set her down. He sat and held her in his lap. "This is scandalous," she told him.

"You like me this way." His wickedness was addicting. He was too correct in his assumption. "Besides, we belong together. It's best that you get used to me keeping you in my lap."

She lifted a brow. "I don't recall agreeing to anything."

"But you will." His confidence should irritate her. "Darling, we're going to get married. Accept it."

"Don't you think you ought to, perhaps, ask me?" Incorrigible arse.

"If you insist." He lifted her hand and kissed her palm. "My love, will you please consent to be my wife and allow me to love you for the rest of our lives? I will endeavor to give you all of myself and ensure you know nothing but pleasure."

Her heart skipped a beat. "I love you. Of course I'll marry you."

"I never thought I could love anyone as much as I do you, my clever little minx." He pressed a kiss to her lips. "We are going to have the best life together."

Emma believed him. Her happiness had never been guaranteed. But now not only was it possible, she would hold on to it with everything she had inside of her. This wasn't a game. She would gladly set that aside for him. There was nothing else she wanted more. Emma held him close and reveled in his embrace. This was the best Christmastide ever. Nothing would ever compare to it.

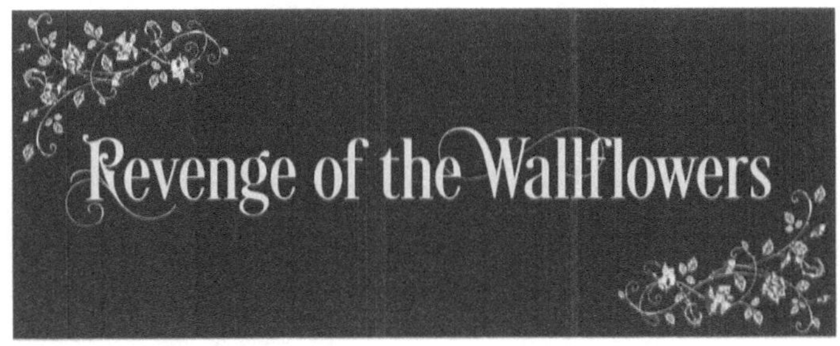

A new book in the Revenge of the Wallflowers' releases each week until March of 2025. Do not miss out on all of these thrilling stories about revenge and love.

Go here and start downloading today!
https://bit.ly/3UMHjBr

Thank you so much for taking the time to read my book.

Your opinion matters!

Please take a moment to review this book on your favorite review site and share your opinion with fellow readers.

www.authordawnbrower.com

Excerpt: A Wallflower's Stolen Christmas

LADY VENGEFUL

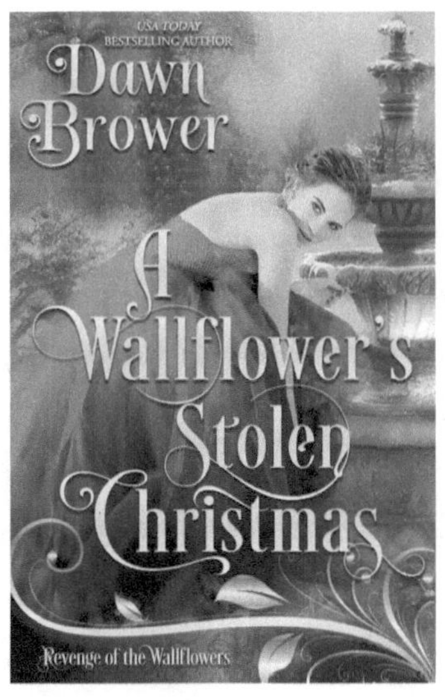

Lady Selena Brooks would much rather remain in the comforts of home during Christmastide. Why the blazes would anyone want to endure a house party for a whole fortnight? Especially one that has always been a wallflower? Society didn't care if she attended, and wouldn't notice her regardless. At least that was how it had been before. Before her cousin restored his finances and set funds aside for her dowry and that suddenly makes her more desirable. Well they could all jump back into the holes they crawled out of. She would never marry anyone that didn't truly appreciate her. Society's dictates had stolen her joy, and the peace of remaining home at Christmas. Selena will stop at nothing to remain unwed, and free from the grips of societal rules. The best revenge is living her life as she truly desires, and she will not let anyone, or more specifically, any *man* ruin her life.

Kingston Rowe, Duke of Castlebury hated society. He wouldn't even attend this house party if he didn't owe one of his friends a favor. He'd only been back in England, after a lengthy absence, for six months, and nothing in society had changed. They were all insufferable fools. One woman stands out amongst them all, and he is riveted with her. She does and says what she wants, but not in malice.

She's kind to the servants and sneers at any gentleman that tries to charm her. He's intrigued, and tempted in ways he never has been before. But how does a duke catch the interest of a woman that doesn't want to be courted?

Prologue

Lady Selena Brooks stared out at the sea of dancers on the floor. Their laughter floated over her in waves of merriment. An emotion that she couldn't feel and hadn't experienced in longer than she could recall. She had, in a lot of ways, been alone her entire life. Her uncle had taken her in as a small child. Not because he had cared about her, but because it had been expected. The previous Earl of Foxcroft, her uncle, had been a wastrel. He'd run his estates into debt and left the responsibility of salvaging it to his son. Selena didn't believe for one moment her uncle had done anything out of the kindness of his heart.

When her father had died, Selena had been left a small inheritance. He hadn't had as much as an earl should have as he was the second son, but it should have left her with a sizable dowry. Her uncle had gambled it all away leaving her with nothing. Now here she was, in her second season, and without any prospects. A wallflower soon to be a spinster if nothing changed. Her gowns had seen better days. Many had been repurposed and redesigned, but there was only so much that could be done. The material on several of her dresses were starting to become threadbare and wouldn't be able to be used much longer.

She was ready to accept defeat. Attending balls and soirees were not helping her cause. There would be no gentleman offering for her. It was time to let that dream die and find a new purpose for her life. Having a family and a home of her own would never happen. No gentleman wanted to take a chance on her. Not with what she had to offer. Apparently, it wasn't enough for them to only take her. They wanted her to have connections and a dowry to offer them. It also didn't matter that she was a beauty. That wasn't arrogance on her part.

Selena looked just like her mother, and during her mother's debut, she'd been the most sought after debutante. But she'd fallen in love with her father and wouldn't consider any other gentleman.

They'd had a love match. Selena remembered that clearly. They had died when she was only ten years old, but before that, her life had been a happy one. She had known joy once. Then it had been ripped away from her and she'd been miserable ever since. In some ways, she had never shaken free from her grief.

Intending to return home after another disastrous evening, she left the ballroom. She was in a hallway leading to the front entrance when a conversation froze her in place. Selena ducked behind an alcove hid from view.

"Have you heard?" a woman said.

"You'll have to be more specific, Lady Darby," the other woman said. "I've heard a great many things."

"The Earl of Foxcroft might actually be a considered a good match soon." She laughed. "Or so my husband has told me. Imagine that—to no longer be a fortune hunter. He's grown his coffers by doing scandalous things. Can you imagine? Doing trade. No gentleman does such things."

They were rude old biddies… Selena ground her teeth together. David was not a fortune hunter. That would imply that he hadn't worked to build the family fortune again. He wasn't quite there yet, though. That was why Selena tried to be as frugal as possible.

"He should have married an heiress," the other woman said. "That's what is done when an earl becomes penniless."

What the hell did they know? David wasn't some dandy that was all right with taking a wife just for her money. Selena had far more respect for her cousin because of his integrity. He had wanted to do this on his own and he'd come so far. Another year, maybe less, and he'd be completely financially stable. He'd already told her that he intended to fully restore her dowry. Not that she cared. She wouldn't want any man that only considered her after she had money to offer for the prospect of marriage.

"Did you see that cousin of his?" The lady said in a dismissive tone. "Why does she bother attending a ball in what is clearly an unfashionable gown? It's pitiable."

And that was why she was done with society. Women like this made her even more miserable with each passing day. She couldn't handle it anymore. It would be far better to retire from the ton forever. She held back a sigh. As much as Selena would like to do that, she knew she couldn't.

David felt guilty for not being able to provide for her. He believed he was at fault for her disastrous seasons. Selena didn't have the heart to disappoint him. So she'd do one more season. Her third season would be her final one.

"It's a shame," the other woman said. "She's a pretty girl. If she'd had a dowry, she'd have been married in her first season. But being a poor orphan didn't help her debut."

She had to leave. She couldn't listen to this for one moment longer. They were in her path to exit the house. There was no helping it. Selena would have to hold her head high and walk past them as if they were not gossiping about her and David. She took a deep, fortifying breath, and then slid out of the alcove.

Selena forced herself to keep a slow, steady pace as she walked down the hall. The two ladies glanced up when they noticed her and thankfully remained silent as she passed by them. Once she reached the front entrance, she had a servant retrieve her shawl for her. She fidgeted as she waited for him to return. When she had her, shawl she wrapped it around her and then left the foyer as quick as possible.

As she had no chaperone, it was easy to slip out of the house and head home. David had escorted her to the ball, but he had been chatting with someone he wanted to do business with. He would be livid she'd left without him, but he'd forgive her. He always did. Her cousin was a dear man. Nothing like the other gentlemen of the ton. Even if one suddenly paid any attention to her, she wouldn't be able to trust it. She didn't want a fickle man as her husband. She'd much rather be a spinster than be married to a man she could never respect.

Society had stolen every chance she had at happiness. The entire lot of them could go to the devil. She didn't need any of them, and by jove, she would prove that to them all. More for herself than anything.

One

Selena leaned against the carriage seat and sighed. She would be arriving at Harcrest Manor soon for this Christmastide house party that Emma insisted on having. If it had been up to her she would have remained home, but instead here she was traveling with her cousin and his wife to a house party. One that would be filled with individuals she loathed. There were very few people that she tolerated. At least all of those she liked would be at this house party. That would make it inherently more tolerable.

Victoria leaned her head on her husband, David, the Earl of Foxcroft's, shoulder and yawned. "I do hope we will be arriving shortly. I'm quite exhausted from the confinement of this carriage."

David patted her arm lightly. "We're all tired, darling. But we should arrive shortly. It's been a while since I've visited Harcrest Manor. It will be wonderful to see our friends."

Selena didn't disagree with her cousin on that regard. Well on any of it really. It wasn't her friends she did not wish to spend time with. It was all the other people that Emma would have invited he had wished to avoid. She'd rather soured to the idea of society and all of its dictates. She wanted to be free from it all, but wasn't certain how to accomplish that feat. What kind of revenge could she enact against society as a whole? Selena did not have one specific target, like Lilah or Cora. Even Victoria had someone specific in mind when she'd targeted David. All three of those ladies had ended up falling in love instead of finding true revenge. She was happy for them. She was…

But she didn't want love or marriage. Not anymore. That dream had died after her first disastrous season. She only attended balls and other societal functions after that because David had been so concerned. He had hoped she'd find a good match. Her dowry during her first two seasons had been pitiful. So she had been mostly overlooked. With her outdated gowns and pittance of a dowry—no man had deigned to pay her any attention. Court-ing? Not even a remote possibility. She might be pretty, but that wasn't enough of an attraction on the husband mart.

"Has Emma told you about her plans?" she asked Victoria.

She shook her head. "I do not know why she wanted a Christmastide house party," Victoria replied. "It will be fun, though. I love house parties."

"As long as you're not the hostess," David drawled. "I seem to recall you complaining about the guest and their tedious requests at the one held at Ardmore."

Victoria wrinkled her nose. "Don't remind me."

"I don't recall that," Selena said. "I thought you enjoyed the house party."

"I didn't hate it," Victoria told her. "But some of the guests were ridiculous. I blame the rain. It had everyone on edge, as we couldn't do any of the planned outdoor activities for a large part of the party. At a Christmastide house party most of the guests will expect more indoor activities."

"Except hunting for a yule log," David reminded her.

Victoria waved her hand dismissively. "That's

for the men to imbibe too much and go traipsing through the snow and otherwise engage in silliness to find some ideal log to cut down, then burn. The ladies will remain inside like any sane person would. We do not need a yule log."

David laughed. "As you can tell," he began. "My wife has strong feelings about yule logs."

"They are not necessary," she told him.

"Not much in life is, love," he said, then kissed her quickly. "That doesn't mean that we shouldn't enjoy anything. You may not find a yule log important, but that doesn't mean you should berate those that do."

"Fine," she said in a reluctant tone. "As I do not have to participate, I see no need to be vocal about it."

Selena sighed. She didn't care either way if the men searched for a yule log. She didn't care about any of it. But still she had to endure conversations like this one. David and Victoria were both dear to her, and she adored them immensely. Their love could be stifling at times. Especially when she couldn't escape the confines of a carriage to be away from it. Selena was so glad that they had found love with each other. Truly. However, as someone that love had skipped over and left alone—it was hard to handle.

"It looks like we're about to turn down the drive to Harcrest Manor," she announced. Selena had been staring out the window for some time now. It was a relief to finally be turning down the drive. Soon they would be at the manor, and she'd be able to escape the carriage.

"Emma will want to meet with us," Victoria said. "As we are all arriving a day before the rest of the guests, I suspect she has a reason for that."

"I gathered as much," Selena replied.

"Do I want to know what you ladies have planned?" David asked as he lifted a brow.

"I wouldn't ask too many questions," Victoria told him. "It's best you do not know."

David had some idea about the revenge pact, but neither Selena nor Victoria had given him much in the way of details. All he knew was that they had decided to help each other have success in society. They just didn't tell him what that success entailed, or how they hoped to achieve it.

"All right," he said. "But do let me know if I may be of assistance. I wouldn't mind aiding the ladies in their endeavors."

Selena almost snorted. He might not be so

ready to help them if he had any idea that they all sought some sort of revenge.

"You are a dear to offer, but that's not necessary." Victoria smiled at her husband. "Just spend this time with your friends."

The carriage came to a stop. Selena nearly bolted from the carriage once a footman opened the door. She didn't wait for Victoria or David. She had other plans. All of which meant some time alone without anyone to bother her.

Selena sighed and entered the sitting room. Victoria, Lilah, and Cora were already there. Where the blazes was Emma. She wanted this little meeting to be done with so she could find her solitude again. "Hello," she greeted the other ladies.

"Hello, Selena," Lilah said. "Come pour yourself a cup of tea. Emma should be here shortly."

Selena walked over to the teacart and prepared her cup, then grabbed a couple biscuits and put them on a plate. She took her tea and biscuits back over to the settee and settled in to wait for Emma.

Emma strolled into the sitting room and

grinned. Selena nibbled on her cookie as she stared at her friend. "Hello," Emma said, then went over to join them. "I'm so happy to see everyone."

Victoria grinned. "We are glad to be here." She patted on the side of the settee next to her. "Come sit. Tell me everything. I want to know your plans."

Emma went over to the settee and sat next to Victoria. She had walked right past the teacart. Did she not want tea? Selena took a sip of her own tea and waited. Perhaps she should be thrilled for Emma to tell them about her revenge plans, but she couldn't find any excitement. She just did not want to be there.

"We all want to know," Cora said, then sipped her tea. "I was excited when the invitation arrived. I suspected this was a scheme of yours. Especially, since Lilah hates socializing." She wrinkled her nose. "Though bravo for having her be the hostess. You know all those harpies are savoring at the opportunity to see if Viscount Harcrest is still besotted with her."

Lilah rolled her eyes. "That man adores me," she said with a contented sigh. "I am truly fortunate to have won his heart. Though if you had asked me that prior to that house party, I would have thought you all mad."

"Indeed," Emma agreed. "The truth is that my brother is the fortunate one. He could have ended up married to the likes of Lady Daisy Allen."

"She's awful," Selena said. "He is indeed lucky that she didn't sink her claws into him." She took a sip of her tea. "Has anyone heard what's happened with her? Anything new?"

"As far as we know," Emma said, then flashed them all an evil grin. "She's still at that finishing school her father sent her to."

Selena was curious about that finishing school. Perhaps she should ask Emma later. She didn't seem to want to share too many details, and she couldn't help wondering why. She tilted her head to the side and mostly listened to the discussion.

"I still think she deserved worse than that," Lilah said. "She nearly ruined my life. All because she thought Henry belonged to her. She was willing to do anything to have him. It's just…wrong."

"It is," Selena agreed. "But she didn't win. That is what you need to remember." She nodded toward Emma. "And that's now why we are here. This house party is for her to get her revenge." She leaned back and stared at Emma. "What do you need from us?" Was it terrible that she hoped that Emma didn't need much from her?

"Nothing," she said. "But I suppose I can tell you my plans. Just in case help is needed, that I haven't already foreseen."

"Go on," Lilah encouraged. "What do we need to know?"

Emma stood and went over to the teacart to pour herself a cup of tea. She put two lumps of sugar into her cup, then stirred slowly. She sighed and went and sat next to Victoria again. Emma sipped her tea and then closed her eyes briefly. When she opened them, they all stared at her, waiting for her to explain it all. "There is much I've told no one," she said. "I mentioned as much to Lilah when we were discussing the invitation."

"You did," Lilah confirmed. "Are you ready to discuss it now?"

"Not entirely," Emma said. "It has to do with my own experience at finishing school. Henry thought it would be good for me to go. I was terribly shy back then. I begged him to let me stay home. In some ways, it helped me to accept myself. I did grow bolder because of my time there." There was pain in her eyes that Selena understood. What had Emma gone through? "But I am afraid I was always destined to be a wallflower."

"What happened to you at school?" Victoria asked.

"It wasn't one thing," Emma said. "A lot happened at school. Some of it I'd rather forget." She inhaled sharply. "But I cannot. It's always there." She glanced away from them. "There were two there that made my life miserable. They are the ones I want revenge on, and I intend to have it."

"Who are they?" Selena asked.

"Yes," Cora said. "We want to know."

Emma shook her head. "Not yet," she said. "When I need your help, I'll let you know. But I want to do this on my own for as long as possible. I need them to understand how their cruelty affected me."

"And you shall," Lilah told her. "Are you going to tell us what you have planned, even if we do not know who?"

She shook her head. "I cannot," she said. "It's too complicated and I am afraid if I start speaking my plans, it will all unravel."

Selena laughed. "All right. Keep your secrets. We will be here if you need us."

In the meantime, Selena would consider what she wanted. Would she try for some sort of revenge? Probably not. She had no need for revenge. Selena just wanted to be herself. Perhaps that was what she would do at this house party. She'd act as she always wanted—society be dammed. Yes. That would be her revenge. If one could call it that. The revenge would be to tell everyone what she thought, whether or not it was socially acceptable, and she would not hold anything back. She'd shock them all so much they wouldn't know how to respond to it. She smiled to herself as she made plans of her own that would be enacted alongside Emma's revenge.

Order Here: https://books2read.com/Wallflow ersStolenChristmas

Excerpt: Her Duke to Savor

LADY BE WICKED

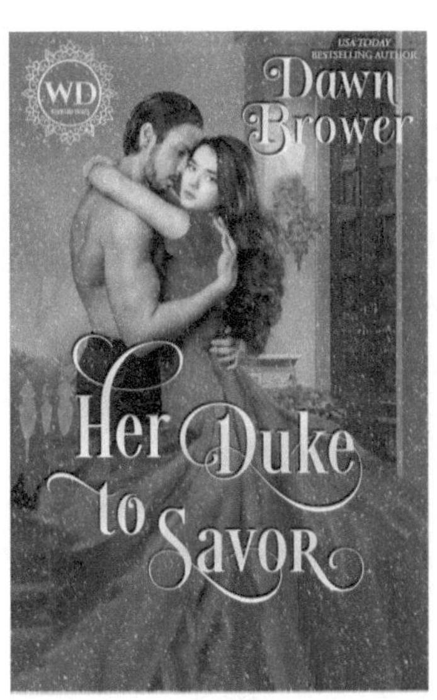

Elias Stevens, the Marquess of Savorton doesn't believe he'll ever fall in love. He may marry one day, because the title demands it; however, that elusive emotion will not be freely given to his future wife.

A house party changes everything for him though. His dearest friend makes a wager with him. He'll fall in love by the new year. Elias takes that bet because he knows his own heart.

Lady Gabriella St. Giles lives a charmed life. She has a good family and fully believes one day she'll mean a gentleman sure to steal her heart. What she doesn't count on is meeting an unsavory marquess at a house party.

Love is on the agenda. One of them wants it and the other hopes to desperately escape it. That wager gives the marquess far more than he could ever imagined, and Gabriella may just acquire her own future duke to savor.

Elias Stevens, the Marquess of Savorton, leaned in his chair and then rocked it on the back two legs as he studied his cards. How many should he discard? After pondering it for a few moments, he set his chair back down on all four legs and leaned on the table. He plucked five cards out of his hand and placed them face down on the table, and then drew five more from the deck carefully arranging them with the ones he still held.

He refrained from grinning at the cards he'd added to his hand. He glanced up at his dearest friend, Elena, the Dowager Countess of Dryden. Her dark red hair shimmered in the candlelight, and there was a gleam in her light gray eyes. She was studying her own cards. The two of them were engrossed in a duel of sorts as they played a grueling game of piquet. This was their last hand in a set of six and would determine which one of them came out the winner. It was a close game and either of them might be declared the victor.

"It's your turn, love," Eli reminded her and tapped a finger impatiently on the table.

"I'm aware," she drawled. "I do not need your guidance." Elena winked. "I'm a far better player than you are."

"Debatable," he replied in an arrogant tone. "I am not so certain you're correct."

Her lips lifted into one of her sensual smiles. It was the type of smile that would set most men aflame with desire, but Eli felt nothing. For him that smile meant something far different. The minx was about to pounce and he would end up metaphorically wounded after she made her strike. Hell. She was going to win, and he didn't like it.

"You always did hate losing," she replied in a glib tone. She removed three cards from her hand and then replaced them with three more from the deck. "There's no need for deliberations. We both know the truth."

"That piquet is a game of chance?" Eli lifted a

brow. "In that you are correct." He refused to admit defeat until he absolutely had to.

She laughed and then grinned at him. "I suppose that is true with any game used for the purpose of gambling. Luck may or may not be on your side." She rearranged her cards in her hand. "But we both know piquet is much more than that. It requires skill, strategy, and an excellent memory. I happen to have all three."

Eli shook his head and sighed and made his declarations, and they continued on with the game. After they were done playing, he had to confess, "I concede, you won." He met her gaze. "I'm not saying you are a better player though."

"Of course you will not. I'd expect nothing less." Her gray eyes sparkled with mischief. "You never have. Why would you change that core part of you now?"

They were at Elena's London townhouse. Many members of the ton believed they were lovers, but nothing could be farther from the truth. Elena and Eli had been friends since they were children. He was only three years older than her, and they first met when he was four and she could barely stand to walk in the nursery. Their mothers had been close and that had brought them together often. Eli was as protective of Elena as he would be if he'd had a sister. When she had married an old man, he had tried to persuade her against the match, but she reminded him they all had their duties to perform and her marriage landed firmly in that column. Her father had arranged the marriage, and she had done as she was told.

Elena had regretted it as her marriage made her miserable. Her husband hadn't been abusive, exactly, but he'd been cold. When she failed to conceive, he'd treated her as if she were a useless person. He may never have physically hit her, but his words were like blows that failed to leave a visible bruise. Eli had never been happier when the earl ceased breathing. When the Earl of Dryden dropped dead suddenly Eli had rejoiced, and secretly so had Elena.

"Do you think you'll ever remarry?" he asked in a noncommittal tone.

She snorted. "Not bloody likely. One marriage of inconvenience is enough to turn me away from such an endeavor." Elena gathered the cards and stacked them neatly on the table. "Why do you ask?"

He didn't want to tell her he'd been thinking about how unhappy she had been. Elena enjoyed being a widow. She had freedom and if she wanted a lover, she could and probably had taken one. Not that, to his knowledge, she did… Eli didn't ask her about anything he didn't really want answers to. "What if you fell in love?"

"That is even more unlikely. Love is a myth they try to make a woman believe." She leaned back and studied him. "Are you in love, Eli?"

"Absolutely not," he said in an emphatic tone. "Unless you count that gorgeous opera singer, I spent an evening with a few nights ago. She was delicious and might convince me I could believe in love."

He was far too busy helping build Savorton Shipping. His family had struggled when he was younger and now that he could, he worked to make their fortune something that rivaled even the most affluent in English society. He was an heir to a dukedom and now the estate thrived. His father had become frail in his old age and left running all the estates to Eli, but still offered input when he felt it was required. Eli did not have time for love.

"A night of passion is not love," Elena replied in a dry tone. "Neither of us is on the market for that elusive emotion."

"So you do not believe you will ever willingly

give your heart away?" This seemed like an opportunity. Should he take it? Elena had never really given any man a chance, and she had good reason for that. As a widow of wealthy means, she didn't have to remarry, but she had a past she seemed determined to forget. One he wanted to remind her about in a subtle way. "You don't have to marry a man if you love him, you know."

"I'm aware," she said, then tilted her head to the side. "I never have to marry again. But you do."

"I've never been married, love," he replied. "I cannot marry again when I never have."

"You are purposely misunderstanding me," she accused. "You know perfectly well what I meant. You're going to be a duke one day and you need heirs."

"I was hoping to convince you to marry me," he said in a smooth tone. "You're the only woman I actually like."

"What a vile thing to suggest." She glared at him. "The very idea of sharing a bed with you..." Elena shuddered.

"Now that wasn't necessary. I'm not revolting." He frowned. She made a valid argument, though. Eli didn't wish to bed her any more than she wanted to join him in that activity.

"Darling," she began as she studied him. "You are passably handsome. I've heard many debutantes expound on your breathtaking visage. Apparently, your black hair and green eyes make them swoon with desire."

"Of course, they do. What they actually desire to be a future duchess, and my gorgeous physique has nothing to do with their admiration." Eli might be a bit jaded... "I am not marrying until I absolutely have to, and love won't be part of the bargain."

"That's too bad," she said in a somber tone. "You're destined to have a marriage like mine."

"I won't be a brute like your husband was. I'd never treat a woman so callously." He wouldn't. Eli had to believe he'd be better than the late Earl of Dryden. Elena was still young and only eight and twenty. She could find someone to be happy with. Somehow, he had to convince her to try.

"Perhaps not," she agreed. "You might be the one that is emotionally abused. I pray you choose wisely."

"I'll have you approve of my future wife." He smiled. "You may have better judgement than me."

"I already do," she said, then laughed. "Perhaps we should make a wager."

It couldn't be that easy… She was playing right into his plans. Elena was a lot like him. She hated to lose. "What sort of wager?"

She tapped on the cards. "All gambling is a matter of chance, but some games are a little more than that. Much like piquet, love can be played in a similar fashion."

"So we use our strategy and skill to avoid falling?" he asked, trying to understand her meaning.

"In a sense," she replied. "We will also have to keep track of all the players, for unlike our little game here, there will be more than two."

"And what exactly is this wager?" Eli asked.

"How about we make it simple," she began. "The first to fall in love by the end of Christmastide loses and owes the other a boon."

He pondered her suggestion. "And what if neither of us falls?"

"Then we both win," she said in a wistful tone. "Or perhaps we will both lose, depending on one's perspective."

Eli doubted he would fall in love. He had yet to meet a woman that inspired such an insipid emotion in him. "All right, I accept. In fact, I have the perfect playing field for us."

She lifted a brow. "Oh?"

"Lady Winston is having a house party. It begins in a couple of weeks and will extend through the entirety of Christmastide. My Mother has been hounding me to attend. I'll tell her I will as long as you go and we can put our wager to the test."

Elena steepled her fingers together. "Excellent," she said in a gleeful tone. "Let the best player win, then."

He was going to enjoy watching her fall, for he knew something she did not. The Earl of Northfield would be in attendance. Elena had never said as much, but the earl had been her first and only love. One she had never had a chance at having a relationship with. Elena had shoved those feelings deep inside her and prepared to marry the Earl of Dryden as her father had ordered. Perhaps this was her second chance at finding happiness.

He wasn't worried about himself. Eli had time to find a suitable wife. His concern was for his dearest friend and helping her find a love she deserved. Besides he hadn't lied, Eli didn't believe in love, at least not when it came to his own life. Love was for other people. Individuals who had the luxury of accepting that gift into their lives. Eli would never be that fortunate.

Acknowledgments

To all my readers. I appreciate you more than I can ever convey. I hope you enjoy this series, and the many more I have planned for you.

About Dawn Brower

USA TODAY Bestselling author, DAWN BROWER writes both historical and contemporary romance. There are always stories inside her head; she just never thought she could make them come to life. That creativity has finally found an outlet.

Growing up, she was the only girl out of six children. She raised two boys as a single mother; there is never a dull moment in her life. Reading books is her favorite hobby, and she loves all genres.

www.authordawnbrower.com
TikTok: @1DawnBrower

BB bookbub.com/authors/dawn-brower
f facebook.com/1DawnBrower
X x.com/1DawnBrower
instagram.com/1DawnBrower
g goodreads.com/dawnbrower

Also by Dawn Brower

HISTORICAL

Stand alone:

Broken Pearl

Connected by a Kiss

A Wallflower's Christmas Kiss

A Gypsy's Christmas Kiss

A Vixen's Christmas Kiss

Marsden Romances

A Flawed Jewel

A Crystal Angel

A Treasured Lily

A Sanguine Gem

A Hidden Ruby

A Discarded Pearl

Marsden Descendants

Rebellious Angel

Tempting An American Princess

How to Kiss a Debutante

Loving an America Spy

Linked Across Time

Saved by My Blackguard

Searching for My Rogue

Seduction of My Rake

Surrendering to My Spy

Spellbound by My Charmer

Stolen by My Knave

Separated from My Love

Scheming with My Duke

Secluded with My Hellion

Secrets of My Beloved

Spying on My Scoundrel

Shocked by My Vixen

Smitten with My Christmas Minx

Vision of Love

Enduring Legacy

The Legacy's Origin

Charming Her Rogue

Ever Beloved

Forever My Earl

Always My Viscount

Infinitely My Marquess

Eternally My Duke

Bluestockings Defying Rogues

When An Earl Turns Wicked

A Lady Hoyden's Secret

One Wicked Kiss

Earl In Trouble

All the Ladies Love Coventry

One Less Scandalous Earl

Confessions of a Hellion

The Vixen in Red

Lady Pear's Duke

Scandal Meets Love

Love Only Me (Amanda Mariel)

Find Me Love (Dawn Brower)

If It's Love (Amanda Mariel)

Odds of Love (Dawn Brower)

Believe In Love (Amanda Mariel)

Chance of Love (Dawn Brower)

Love and Holly (Amanda Mariel)

Love and Mistletoe (Dawn Brower

The Neverhartts

Never Defy a Vixen

Never Disregard a Wallflower

Never Dare a Hellion

Never Deceive a Bluestocking

Never Disrespect a Governess

Never Desire a Duke

Lady Be Wicked/Wayward Dukes'/Wicked Widows'

Her Rogue for One Night (Wicked Widows)

A Lady Never Tells

Her Duke to Beguile

Her Duke of Sin (Wayward Dukes')

Her Duke to Savor (Wayward Dukes')

Coming in 2024/2025

A Lady Never Confesses

A Lady Never Forgets

Her Rogue for Christmas (Wicked Widows)

Her Rogue to Kiss Good Morning (Wicked Widows)

Her Duke to Seduce (Wayward Dukes')

Her Duke to Tempt (Wayward Dukes')

CONTEMPORARY

Stand alone:

Deadly Benevolence

Snowflake Kisses

Kindred Lies

Sparkle City

Diamonds Don't Cry

Hooking a Firefly

Novak Springs

Cowgirl Fever

Dirty Proof

Unbridled Pursuit

Sensual Games

Christmas Temptation

Daring Love

Passion and Lies

Desire and Jealousy

Seduction and Betrayal

Begin Again

There You'll Be

Better as a Memory

Won't Let Go

Heart's Intent

One Heart to Give

Unveiled Hearts

Heart of the Moment

Kiss My Heart Goodbye

Heart in Waiting

Heart Lessons

A Heart Redeemed

YOUNG ADULT FANTASY

Broken Curses

The Enchanted Princess

The Bespelled Knight

The Magical Hunt